HUMAN RIGHTS

UNDEAD SET ON LIVING

DAMON
RATHE

Fishcake Publications

Human Rights
(Undead Set on Living)

Published by Fishcakes Publications

www.fishcakepublications.com

ISBN 978-1-909015-27-2
Paperback Edition

First Edition Published in Great Britain in April 2016.

Cover Illustrations by Martin Rothery.

Contents

Prologue

It's not my fault that I'm undead.

At least I don't think it is.

Don't you pick on me just because I'm mortally challenged. In the pre-apocalyptic society, I could have taken you to court for discrimination over that. Now, however, human law seems to be governed by whoever has the most guns and controls the most water. But that is fine, I don't need water, it tends to go straight through me these days, and I don't need a gun either, I am an immortal, relentless, tireless killing machine (as long as no-one removes my head of course).

So what motivates me, you may ask? Well today, it is my intention to find some surviving humans and either eat their brains or convert them into one of my kind. Preferably the ones without guns, they can be a bit annoying.

I sometimes wonder why humans are so precious about going on living. As far as I can tell, there's probably not many of them left. Supplies and food are dwindling and our numbers continue to rise, so it's only a matter of time before our fully organised campaign takes the rest of them with us into never-ending oblivion.

I know, I know, oblivion sounds a bit final and dramatic, but it's not as bad as it sounds. You see, this objective needs to be achieved if zombie society is to move forward and progress. Yes, progress.

We can't fling ourselves against bullets, weapons and artillery forever, that would just be foolish, it has to stop sometime. Let me tell you, I take no pleasure in having to batter down defences and scare the human folk witless with my non-stop, fear inspiring, and mindless determination. I only moan out loud because that is what is expected, so stereotypical, although I suppose it could be because I'm just so fed up with the whole situation.

Besides, I've found there are a number of benefits to being undead. For starters, I don't have to shave anymore (I hated that), and I don't have that bad back either, in fact I don't have a bad anything anymore. That is unless you consider the dry, flaky skin, the oozing orifices and occasional limb falling off when hit by a weapon, but you get used to it. Well, except the limb thing of course, that can be quite a nuisance, especially if it's a leg. You never see a hopping zombie, well, not in public anyway. Touch wood, I've been lucky so far.

So, it's time to leave my dark hole of a basement, get out into the cold, wet night and harvest some humans. I still haven't figured out why I don't like the light anymore, I don't venture out at all during the day, I've been told not to. It's like being a child again, being told what to do. It's not like there's a risk of sunburn or anything with dead skin, is it? I'll have to remember to ask my recently undead welfare counsellor about that, see if he knows why.

Maybe he can also tell me why we need to eat brains. It's not as if I have a working digestive system anymore is it? Or need to create the energy to live and the nutrition to replenish my cells. However, they are incredibly addictive and I don't know why. But, as he keeps drumming into us, I should do my bit for the common good and work for a better undead society and it appears eating brains is one of our main goals. That is as well as wanton destruction and causing a very bad smell. A stench, of course, we can't even detect, but we know the humans hate it, even if the advance of a bad waft gives us away and let them know we're coming. It does repel them a bit, although I wish it did the same for the flies, they are starting to get annoying now. Oh look, there's Wobbling Bob, he was once my neighbour and got turned about the same time as me. Total coincidence, we were miles apart at the time, but it's always nice to see a familiar face isn't it? He's recently had his throat ripped out by a rabid dog, he can't even moan anymore. An unfortunate incident, but you do have to be careful when you smell like rotting meat. In fact, rabid dogs are probably the only animals that come near us anymore. The rest run away like they've smelled a forest fire.

We must be on the same squad tonight. We've been given an assignment just on the outskirts of this city (don't ask me which one, they all look the same now – totally destroyed). This is a campaign that's been going for quite some time now. There's a band of humans holed up on an estate, they've set up barricades and everything. It's rumoured some of them are ex-military, and they've been raiding into other areas of the city and setting fire to our hideouts, trying to wipe us out. They're a bunch of terrorists, that's what they are, fighting against our democratic majority. Just because they are now a minority people and haven't joined us to get their vote, doesn't mean they can spread their anarchy just to win back their insignificant human rights.

Apparently, our hierarchy has had enough, so we've been sent in to negotiate an end to the hostilities to the best of our ability. As it happens, our best tactic at negotiation is to either eat their brains or just bite and infect them enough to persuade them into coming round to our way of thinking.

I think it's marvellous how one tiny bite can really change the way you think towards undead society.

I remember, back in the day, when people would try and fight off the invading host of zombies from their homes while trying to protect their family from what they thought was a ravenous horde thirsty for their blood and bring an unnatural end to their lives.

They weren't happy at all, these families. They could hardly be provided for. The mains and river water was polluted with the zombie virus, they had little food, there was no heating or electric, you couldn't even light a fire without giving away your position. They became so tired; barely had enough strength to fight us off.

My last moments are very distant. It gets harder and harder to try and recall them, my savage side and base instincts seems to have taken over.

I think there were three of us, me, my wife and my son, who had all incurred injury and several bites after fleeing into the woods. The changes were slight at first, a slight greying of the skin, red eyes, and the itchiness, closely followed by the dire thirst for…something…and then the rotting began.

I used to get so irritated by the itchy skin and gangrenous limbs, but after a while, when you realise there's nothing you can do about it, you soon learn to accept your fate. Once we'd turned we were accepted with open rotting arms into the collective. Our unexplainable bloodlust and hunger brought us back to the city under the care of some very helpful zombies that just seemed to know where we were, but underlying that seemed to be an inner calling bringing us into the society of our new kind. A homing instinct, if you like, to be part of the big society.

My wife now has a cushy job stockpiling brainless bodies in the sewer away from all the violence, so I know she'll be happy with that. Not quite sure what my son does now, but I believe he's been drafted into some elite incursion unit because of his size. It's easier for the smaller ones to get through grates and underground pipes, that sort of thing. I bet he's having a great time; he was always getting into that sort of mischief.

Ah, we're getting a bit closer to the compound now. Stockpiled cars, makeshift fences – no problem. It takes a while when you have to mostly drag yourself around, but we get there eventually. Ok, I may not be able to feel pain anymore, but the downside is that your body just doesn't work the way it used to. Sometimes it's a bit frustrating. I can manage a respectably fast shuffle nowadays, though my arms are still pretty flimsy when I walk. Poor Wobbling Bob over there, his limbs are a bit twisted and he's developed rather a nasty limp, probably because of that in-turned foot. But you don't hear him complaining, he just gets on with it. Good for him.

Oh dear, the people in the compound have lit torches, this could get a bit nasty. I don't like fire much; it has a habit of burning off your flesh and, being undead, I can't regenerate mine. I know it doesn't hurt, but it's a bit embarrassing when you get home in front of the lads and all your innards are showing or parts of you are flaking away. You never hear the end of it. Ah, looks like they've got some big guns as well. Silly humans, they never learn. They should know by now that they only slow us down, you can't kill us (unless they get a lucky headshot, of course). But most of them are civilian and don't know how to use them properly, they couldn't hit a barn door from ten yards. I'll have to be careful though, I don't fancy losing any limbs today, it's bad enough dragging my carcass around as it is without having to do it with only my arms or only my legs. I prefer to get out and about a bit. I've got a friend back at the pit, Post-top Carl, who's literally just a head now. He keeps saying he's alright, but to be honest, he seems a little depressed now he's got no body.

The first wave's just gone in. They're a bunch of nutters, them lot. It really is nice of them, though, to take the brunt of it like that, they really are looking after the rest of us at the back, the novices, if you will. Ha ha, that flimsy fence didn't stop them, did it? I can hear the screams now, and...yep, there's the gunfire. Oi, steady on, that bullet's just taken off my big toe. It's bad enough shuffling along as it is without having to stumble as well. You just wait till I get my teeth into you, you bugger, with your lucky shot.

Oh no, poor Wobbling Bob's just taken a hit with a flaming arrow, he's not going to be happy about that. Get down and roll Bob before it really catches. He's just carrying on, what a trooper! But not too bright, though.

Right, now I'm here, let's find a victim; I need to make my allocated contribution to the proceedings. It's a bit chaotic at the moment, can't see for all this smoke. The gunfire seems to have abated, that's good news. Looks like the humans are all corralled into the one building in the corner; I can just see the ends of the guns sticking out from between the boards across the windows.

Now, how many of us are still standing? About one and a half thousand, well that should do it, I think there's only a few of them left. We've always got numbers on our side. Soon have them boards down and we can all pour in through the window, like a mouldy, fleshy flood.

Wait a minute, what's that over there, in the shadows, behind those unlit windows. It looks like…yes, it is, women and children trying to escape. It would appear that the men are trying to buy them some time by drawing us towards their position. Well, we can't be having that, can we? C'mon lads, this way, there's a bunch of easy targets over here. We mustn't discriminate now.

Need maximum shuffle speed here, probably be able to catch them by surprise as I…heave…there you go, one collapsed door. This place is a death-trap. Oh look, no other way out of the room, hee hee. Stop screaming please, you're making a right racket.

Now we can do this the easy way or the hard way, as me and my friends here just want to either turn you into useful members of our society or eat your brains, that's all. Let me say, it's your choice, let it not be said that zombies aren't fair.

Oh I see, it's going to be like that is it madam? You really think that you can slash me across my chest with that kitchen knife and expect no consequences? You thug. Stop struggling; I'll lose my grip on your head. Ah, there you go, one big squeeze and off comes the top. Ooh, look a big, grey squishy one, I bet you were quite intelligent once looking at the size of it. Not any more, eh? I'll put that one in my pocket, save that one for later. Maybe it will cheer Carl up a bit? Oh, go on then, just a quick bite, he won't notice.

Who's next? A little girl? Not much of a fight there. Aw, she's crying, backed helplessly into a corner. How sweet. Don't worry little girl, let me give you a quick bite, I'll take all your fears away. Ack, a bit bony, I'll just leave her there until she turns later.

It's gone a bit quiet outside. No shooting, shouting, screaming or banging…it must be over. Seems many of my colleagues here have got to the remaining humans, that's excellent. Finished in good time tonight without hardly any casualties to us. Even good old Bob is happily feasting on a brain over there, though he looks a bit worse for wear, a bit scorched. The fire seems to have been put out by the amount of blood he's drenched in. It is funny watching all that gore fall out through his severed throat, but he's so happy he hasn't even noticed, bless him.

Oh, looks like a few of the advanced lot took quite a few casualties after all, there's a lot of headless corpses over their by that main door. Have the humans finally found our weakness after all? Bit late for that, eh?

Well that was another good night's work, best be getting back now, before it gets light. Probably take a bit longer now I've got a missing toe, I do feel a bit unbalanced. I've also got a meeting with my shift supervisor at five o'clock in the morning for a performance review. Apparently, these are mandatory after three months, but I think I've done pretty well considering I've only been undead for that long.

I'll give Post-top Carl some brains, and then settle down for the day after that. I'm sure we have another human settlement scheduled in for tomorrow; our work will never be done until we've eliminated all the humans it seems.

I really should write some of this stuff down, shouldn't I? Or pass this knowledge on in some sort of story, keep a journal maybe. Can I still write? I'd have to go back a bit though and tell it from the beginning otherwise much of this won't make any sense to anyone. But where would I begin…

<u>Fitting In</u>

The recent itching seems to have stopped now which, I think, is a good thing, or maybe one bad depending on how you look at it. It indicates my nerves are probably all dead now. All feeling is gone. It feels a bit weird, actually. It's like I know I'm there, but I can't feel myself. A floating conscience.

Not breathing has to be the strangest thing; it seems so unnatural, against nature itself. I can move, but I'm not even sure how I'm managing that. There's no blood running through my body; that all appears to have congealed and occasionally it oozes out of cracks or breaks in my skin like black treacle. Amazing.

How is my brain even working when it's not being fed by blood and oxygen? Heck, I'm not even going to think about that: oh, I just did. Mmm. Stop it, I'm confusing myself.

Also, another thing I don't understand – why am I so hungry now? Almost ravenous. I don't think I need to consume for sustenance any more as my metabolism doesn't work, but I seem to have this never ending craving for something bloody, watery, meaty, squishy and soft but I'm not quite sure what. I'll have to find out what that's all about.

Luckily, we have our induction shortly and I believe they are going to fill us in on everything we need to know, so hopefully some of my questions will be answered then. Some of the others here have heard rumours that what they show and tell you can really distress you, but you can't tell if anyone is being serious as everyone now only has one expression on their face and that seems to be the one you die with. It's amazing how much we actually relied on facial expression to communicate, that's no good now. Now, we're a right bunch of grisly expressions which range from surprise to absolute pain.

I have to admit, becoming a zombie is not at all what I expected. Everything is so organised, it's beyond belief. The last thing I would've imagined as that grotesque, mutilated, hideous thing (who I now guess is my un-birth father) staggered towards me among the seething mass and bit me, is that he, and they, were doing it for a cause.

Yes, they have a cause. We have a cause.

A democratic system, a collective society and one with ambition.

And apparently that's what I'm going to learn about today.

I really hope I can fit in, not sure what they do with you if you don't? Hope my family fits in as well. It will help us all come to terms with our new situation. It's been a while since I've seen them; I wonder where they have gone. I was told that this was for my own good, separating me from my family, as sometimes it's not so pleasant seeing someone else going through the change, especially loved ones. So we were split up, to be spared the heartache during the transition time, watching our nearest and dearest start to rot and putrefy. Who'd have thought zombies would have feelings towards suffering? I heard from one of the new lads that it can unbalance you a little, too much for the recently turned mind to cope with. Apparently, there's a quarry somewhere containing all the unhinged; ones that can't let go of their former lives and keep trying to commit suicide. Of course, this would never work as one you have become undead, killing yourself becomes a bit more complicated, so this freaks them out even more as you can probably understand. They are just left in a deep pit for their own safety - and ours. Imagine that - a pit of despair.

Oh, here we go, we're being summoned. Through those big, heavy, and menacing looking doors. That's a bit dramatic. Was that screaming I just heard? There's not many here today, just eight of us. Must be more than one training session because I'm sure they brought dozens here last night, all brought in like battery farm chickens. Three women, rest of us men. At least, I think some are men, bit difficult to tell with a couple of them. Looks like they put up a bit of a struggle towards the ends, all sorts of bits missing. That chap over there looks like the remains of a raw burger he's got that many teeth marks on him. That must really have itched, and the worst thing is that you can't scratch either, otherwise you start knocking all sorts of lumps off – not nice.

So, who's this then? He looks a bit official. He's got a uniform on so he must be important, and he's almost clean. Mustn't have seen much action this fellow, which can only mean one thing – he's a bureaucrat, one of the backroom boys with a cushy number going on. Oh, he's our supervisor; it seems, just as bad I suppose. And who's this coming in? Counsellor for the recently deceased? Really? Are you kidding me? What's he for? Am I expected to have a big cry and express all my innermost feelings? Well, I'm a bit angry right now. I'm pretty sure this isn't the career I would have chosen for myself. I guess I better listen to what they have to say.

Welcome? Ok, thank-you, but I don't think I had much of a choice, did I? Hope we fit in and enjoy our time with the organisation and become a valuable, productive member of zombie society? We'll have to see about that, won't we? Become a contributing and valuable member of the team? Hang on, this sounds like work to me. The big rousing speech given to brainwash new employees as they come on board. At least they can't work us to death, or more likely bore us to death for that matter.

Hang on! This is worse.

We'll have to work forever! Or at least until we fall apart. That pit of despair is looking more and more inviting.

So, it seems our aim is to grow zombie society for the advancement of our race. We are all equal and will all be rewarded in the end - it seems some are more equal than others, eh, desk jockey? This is starting to sound like government propaganda to me. They'll be teaching us a weird salute next.

Now, the company mottos. 'Brains'. 'Kill all humans'.

How original.

They must have taken ages coming up with those. Isn't it annoying when un-life starts imitating the movies. The last one's a bit of a strange one though, as surely, we don't want to kill them all, otherwise how do we create more of us? Seems like a bit of a paradox to me. I'll have to put that one to the supervisor later, see what company spiel they come back with on that one. Bet they've got an answer for everything this lot. In fact, how long before they hand out the employee handbook? Now, I know I haven't been a zombie for long, but come on; this is all starting to sound worse than being dead. I might as well become a robot. They are just trying to brainwash us. What are we really going to achieve? If we really rid the planet of all the humans, there'll be no-one left to convert so our population will become static. Then what will we do? Turn on each other? Build something further? Evolve? Who knows? I guess we'd probably just rot away – what a glorious end for civilisation! But if we don't try to kills humans, then they are obviously going to try and annihilate us. For some reason, they really don't like us. I should know; I used to be one. No doubt because we keep trying to eat their brains and bite them, they seem to find that annoying. Well, who wouldn't? Perspectives soon change around here, though.

Could our races ever live together in harmony? Mmm, not looking at the faces of this lot they're bringing in. Captured humans. They look terrified. Well, we must look pretty grisly, I'm not surprised.

So what's going on now? Training? What sort of training requires live humans? Whoa, look, one of them is trying to get away. Blimey, those two zombies were on him like a shot. Ooh, that looked painful. Aw, come on guys; eat with your mouths closed, you're dribbling blood all over the place. No wonder they think we're disgusting. Those other humans won't taste as good now; they've gone all white and tense. Was this the hunger I'd been feeling? Oh hang one, I can't taste anymore now; can I. Hey, what's the point in having a craving if you can't satisfy it with the taste of something. I'll never get rid of it.

Stop crying humans, you'll be one of us soon and you'll have to go through all this so you might as well pay attention. Won't they? Wait, we have to what? Oh, I see, it's a practical training session. Oh dear. You're trying to drive the last fragments of humanity out of us, aren't you?

So, two each. What do we do? Follow the supervisor's lead. Right, stop wriggling human. Oh, I'm so sorry, this is going to hurt. Grab scalp, grab chin. I said stop wriggling! Then twist. Glad my ears don't work as well any more, that's some screaming. Soon stop that. Oops, softer than I thought, I'm stronger than I knew, my fingers have gone straight through. Damn it, blood makes everything so slippery, I've dropped the body on the floor and, aw no, the lovely brain has fallen on the floor as well.

Why did I just think 'lovely brain' just then? Is that what I've been craving? I think it is.

A quick wipe on my sweater should do it, can't blow the muck off now. Then again, maybe not, I'm dirtier than the floor. Oh well, it's not like I can get ill from this, is it?

Mmm, chewy, yet tender. Hint of iron. Gosh, I can taste it. I didn't expect that. If I could do it, I think I'd drool. Hang on, I am. How's that happening?

I need more. I need more. Come here second human specimen. Eh? Why? What do you mean I can't have her brains as well? Stupid supervisor. I want it, I want it, I want it. No, I'm not prepared to settle for her body, I want her mind. Ooh, clever, this must be their tactic for obedience, they're getting us all hooked, and it's working. The worse thing is, I know it's working and I don't care. It's like the reverse of drug rehab. So what do I do with this one? Bite her? Ok. Create a zombie. I suppose it makes a change to destroying life all the time. Although, I think I would rather be the brainless fella on the floor right now. Wait, does this make me a father again?

Bringing a new zombie unlife into the world? That reminds me;
I wonder how my wife and son are getting on? The missus will
hate this, she was a vegetarian and my boy was a blood fainter,
so I can only imagine how he's taking it. Although, you never
know, one bite of those nice, juicy, tasty brains might change
their minds. Need more brains, need more brains, urgh…I think
I'm hooked.

Aw, don't take the bodies away, I was enjoying that. I think I
was anyway, though I can't be sure. I feel a little…guilty? Yes,
guilty. Just wasting human life like that, what was the point?
What was achieved? Oh, they're going to tell us now are they?
These are regular feelings for newly inaugurated zombies and
we're bound to have many moral questions and dilemmas
during the transition period that is why the counsellor for the
recently undead was introduced.

Marvellous.

We're all getting an initial appointment and can make
subsequent appointments as we see fit or are required.

So, we've had killing training and we're going to have a mental
medical. Are we being drafted into an army of darkness? It feels
that way.

No, it's a democracy is it? Well, I didn't expect that. Our region
votes for a councillor, does it? Then these councillors sit on a
board and elect a national representative to be part of a
government. Well that sounds quite impressive, but what do
they govern exactly? Ah, it seems they are responsible for
planning the world domination in the war against humans and
organising our roles within society. So it seems the members of
the government do in undeath exactly what they did in life –
absolutely nothing and talk a lot making stupid decisions. But,
in the end, I suppose it's nice to be the ones choosing who does
nothing – democracy in action.

Counsellor for the Recently Deceased

I was feeling a bit overwhelmed.

The gravity of what they were asking us to do had finally struck home. I was killing people, or if not killing them, condemning them to a life they hadn't actually chosen. Who was I to determine how these people continued to exist?

Yes, zombie society may be ordered and well run with the aim of creating a better world for us all, but who has the right to tell everyone that's what they want? To be dictated to, told how to live their un-life. We are all cogs in a big machine now and I was starting to register something within that I couldn't quite fathom. It was a strange feeling, something akin to having trapped wind but confined to thought alone, as my physical body didn't do that anymore.

Well that wasn't strictly true. The brains and flesh I consumed did cause a lot of gas and I wasn't immune from the occasional raspberry style discharge as the bacteria breeding within me rotted down the contents of my guts.

Anyway, whatever it was, I wasn't feeling very comfortable.

So, I'd made an appointment with the counsellor for the recently deceased who we all called Shrunken Head Sean. It seemed to fit. Especially since the day he'd been out in the sun too long. Dried up like a sultana, he did.

He obviously felt some kind of importance and therefore had his own room. Ok, it was an old broom cupboard, but he had at least two square yards worth of space to himself, unlike the rest of us that dwelt in a darkened basement virtually shoulder to shoulder.

So we stood facing one another in the tight, dark space, as the door was closed, gently swaying from side to side. He was studying me as much as I was studying him. He'd obviously had hundreds, if not thousands, of others through that door. I wondered what qualified him for this job. Was a shrink in his life before? That would be no good as no-one can remember their lives from before. Was he more experienced than us? Had he been doing this for an exceptionally long time and seen it all? I guess I would find out. However, he dealt with those of us that couldn't cope with change, those that couldn't go through with it and those that couldn't conform to society or just couldn't get their heads around this crazy society and the role that that they had landed in it.

I was wondering where he thought I fit in.

I had issues of doubt and non-conformity, somewhere inside I seemed to know that killing so many humans was wrong despite them being the enemy. I could see the paradox. I couldn't rationalise the fact that our government was so happy to order thousands of us to strike at them, many of our kind being destroyed in the process, on a whim. That hardly felt like building a society to me. Add this to the fact that we were being quantified on our achievements and it seemed like an extra stress to add to the brain when still trying to cope with all these questions. Not to mention my newly found addiction to brains. I put all this to the counsellor.

In turn, I could sense confusion from him. Why was he studying me like that? As if asking questions is not a normal thing to do? Had I done something wrong in having concerns?

After several more minutes of swaying and eyeballing one another in the dark, he seemed to come to a conclusion. To this day I still can't believe the advice he gave to me. When I had all these queries and rebellious feelings all dying to be answered, the response I got still amazed me.

When I stood with my back to the closed door, I asked myself – what does he mean I'll get over it?

I guessed I would have to find my own answers from then on. He was bloody useless!

A Friend Returns

It hadn't stopped raining for two bloody days.
Although it had started gently at first, more of a shower, it was
now coming down in torrents. I mean, blanket rain. Stood here
at the arched gate, temporarily sheltering, I could barely see
the church only a hundred yards away, a mere blur I the near
distance.
In the soggy graveyard of St Agatha's in the Vale, family,
friends and colleagues gathered closely around the open grave
of the late doctor Andrew Farnham to say their goodbyes. Well
as closely as they could, anyway, without bumping brollies.
Andy was a long term colleague and very close friend of mine,
arguably my best friend. We'd come up through the labs
together, right from our college and university days, but
recently he'd been working on something secret. So secret, he
couldn't even tell me, his best friend. How come I could know
the exact moment guy lost his virginity, yet when I questioned
him about this new work he would always change the subject
or steer the conversation in another direction. It had to be
government or military work, that's what I would guess
anyway, it was all so hush hush.
His wife looked so tense, and no wonder, he'd been in some
kind of accident at work and his 'employer' wasn't divulging
any details about what happened. So, here we were, in this
damp cemetery, full of sorrow, anger and suspicion with the
loss of a good friend and a lot of unanswered questions.
Huddled together in grief and the natural need for
companionable shelter raindrops struck down like drumbeats
on our umbrellas sounding their own funeral dirge. This was
accompanied in harmony by the ever present whoosh, splash

and gurgle of the swelling river that ran alongside the cemetery.

To our concern, it was rapidly rising.

We could barely hear the reverend's words of comfort above the thrum of precipitation as the coffin was, a bit too quickly I thought, lowered into a six inch deep pool of muddy water, resulting in a big splash at the bottom of the six foot hole. The ropes were slick with rainwater. You could see the embarrassment on the men's faces, it wasn't a professional performance. However, it wasn't their fault, these were hardly normal conditions.

Lightning flashed across the sky and immediately thunder roared as the sky darkened deeper, a grey shade violet, heralding another even heavier downpour probably with more thunder and lightning. Everyone gathered, jumped, and then pulled closer together seeking whatever protection they could. Ironically, I felt quite pleased with myself for remembering to bring my wellies, they weren't all laughing now. Not that this was an occasion that warranted humour. But Andy would have got it.

Abruptly, we all turned in unison towards a sudden commotion, audible even over the drone of the rain, caused by the undertaker who had been patiently stood off to one side with the hearse. He was running towards us, slipping in the mud as he did so, waving and shouting something, a look of panic and urgency on his face; however we still couldn't make out what he was saying. Yet it didn't take us long to figure out as he was being followed by a huge swell of knee deep water rushing across the ground. The river had burst its banks and was beginning to sweep over the cemetery. Brown murky water advanced on us ominously.

'Everyone to the church, please, it's on higher ground,' shouted the reverend. We all heard that well enough, no need to tell us

twice, and began to squelch our way hastily towards the old
stone building on top of a steep rise.

Younger people were helping the older ones up the sharp
incline whilst all the time we could see the tide line advancing
towards us. Running us down.

Glancing back, I saw it had it started to swallow gravestones
on the lower slope, washing away memories of the dead,
making its way towards us and, with horror, I suddenly
realised, towards Andy's open grave.

I stood in disbelief as the water reached its edge and cascaded
over the lip with a splash, a glug, pouring into the six foot hole.
The water was quickly up to ground level sickeningly bringing
with it the coffin which, with a gloop, bobbed up to the surface
and started to float towards us on the advancing wave like a
Goth's surfboard.

'Andy! He's floating away. Can't you do something?' I shouted
at the undertaker and the reverend who were just looking back
at me with questioning, stunned faces, aghast that anything
like this could actually happen. I was pretty sure there wasn't
even a biblical precedent for this. Try and pass this one off as
God's will. They were obviously used to putting them down
holes, not watching them come back up again.

'Damn it,' I muttered as I started wading out through the
shallows to the ever deepening water towards the floating
coffin that had now got lodged on a cross shaped gravestone.
Somebody had to do something. I was determined to restore
some dignity to these proceedings and I didn't want my old
friend washing away. The thought disgusted me.

What had started as a finely polished cherry wood and silver
metal casket now resembled more of a shipwreck that had
washed ashore as I finally caught hold of one of the handles
and managed to drag it toward the makeshift shoreline. The

river water had seemed to find its level now and the rest of the congregation awaited its abatement on the temporary bank.

'You always said you wanted to go on a cruise, Andy,' I joked. 'Bet you didn't think it would like this.'

Suddenly, I heard a noise. More of a scratching really. But I couldn't figure out where it was coming from because the gush of water mixed with the splashing of the rain was playing tricks on my ears. Then I realised with horror – from the coffin. Movement within?

Could it be?

'He's still alive, he's still alive! He's drowning. Help. Help me get this open. We have to get him out!'

The undertaker who'd finally closed his gaping mouth eventually came over to help and prised open the lid. A small gush of water poured out. The corpse of Andrew Farnham still lay there, wet, but very still, but with his hands facing upwards – weird. As I examined him again, I realised they'd done well to hide the bite marks.

I fell to my knees with a splash as the memories and grief came flooding back.

'Must have been the water leaking in that made the noise, sir. Bubbles or something. The body floating within was probably banging against the lid. Sorry.' The undertaker didn't seem convinced.

'Oh, Andy. I'm so sorry, mate,' I whispered. What was wrong with me, of course he was dead. Wishful thinking wasn't going to bring him back as sure as river water wasn't going to resurrect him like some holy baptism.

Andy's wife had come over to see what all the fuss was about and on seeing her dead husband again fell to her knees by his side, sloshing in the mud, mindless of her new, black dress. Sobbing quietly, she took his cold, wet, limp hand in hers – when it suddenly tightened.

Andy's wife's hand was caught in a vice like grip. She screamed a terrifying, haunting scream of pure fear. Horrified, she desperately tried to pull away, urgently yanking and tugging, but it was held fast. I went to help, trying to pry those dead fingers off but there was no chance, they were locked with almost inhuman strength.

Then Andy's eyes popped open, milky and pale. A loud moan came from his mouth making us all jump.

Andy's wife screamed again and in the panic I slipped backwards in the mud falling flat on my backside.

Like a spring-loaded catapult, pivoted at the waist, Andy bolted upright pulling his snare victim towards him and sank his teeth into his wife's face, taking a good chunk of the cheek and the chin, and blood poured out. The perpetual screaming of shear terror chilled me more than the freezing rain and an overriding instinct overwhelmed telling me to get away from this imminent danger as quickly as possible.

What had happened to him? What was this inhuman thing emerging from the coffin? I wasn't staying around long to find out.

I'm ashamed to say, I turned and ran. But then, so did everybody else.

I didn't know what that was back there, but it wasn't Andy, and it had just feasted his wife. I didn't want to know anymore. Andy had been replaced by a monster and that scared the life out of me. I felt sick. I heaved but nothing came out. The sooner I was away from here, the better.

I'd come to terms with it later.

Home Sweet Home

I know it's not much, but hey, at least we can call it a home of sorts. We're quite lucky really because this warehouse basement only houses around a thousand of us and I reckon it could easily fit in another hundred, so we've got plenty of space.

Do you know, at the end of a long night marauding, terrorising, dismembering, converting humans (as much as possible to reach my quota, of course) and eating brains, it's nice to get back and relax during those nasty daylight hours and just gently sway amongst your fellow undead. Not only is it physically gruelling, but mentally as well.

Many of these guys are starting to feel like family now, some close bonds are forming. Although sometimes you can forget who is who, mainly due to the fact that many of them can come back with either fewer limbs, missing skin or damage caused by fire or bullets. We laugh about it, those of us who have mouths of course, to keep the spirits up. I say laugh, comes out more like a high pitch moan, bit like a whoopee cushion.

I managed to ask my supervisor why we can only go out at night whilst having my three month evaluation meeting. It seems so long since I saw the sun. I know I wouldn't be able to bask in its warmth, but it does bring back a few happy memories, even though it seems to be considered as fiery evil by many of my co-workers. Apparently, and to my surprise, it turns out we can go out without harm during the day. But as a relatively recent undead, I just haven't earned that work privilege yet. I couldn't believe it, a work privilege? We even get told when we can and cannot go outside now? How unfair! Apparently, I will have to get my numbers up for work perk. Although, Post-top Carl states it's not much of a privilege because you're an easier target in daylight, I think that's how he lost his body and he's slightly bitter about it.

Looking back, my evaluation didn't go as well as I thought it would, in fact it was very disappointing. I thought I was fitting in so well, but it appears not. It seems one kill and one conversion just isn't enough. Well, they have put me on the back row, what do they expect? And it was my first night. Those frontliners were grabbing all the glory and not leaving much for the rest of us. Apparently, I need to pull my finger out a bit more. Not literally, of course, I'm trying to keep all my limbs as long as possible, can't do with losing a digit. You need a good grip to dismember the heads. The supervisor says I need to do more and has given me what he calls 'an achievable target'. A target! Like it's some sort of human conversion factory where will they give themselves willingly, I think not. Doesn't he know they might just resist a little? Not to mention the weaponry they like to bear upon us.

I'll do my best of course, but I admit, I'm not finding it easy. I tried to explain that I am new at this and that I have these nagging feelings that seem to stem from my mortal past that are inhibiting me slightly, making me hesitant to take a life.

After a twenty-two minute lecture on the core values of zombie society, delivered rather aggressively I thought, I was sent away to really think about how I would like to progress and develop in the future and to practice my mantras 'brains' and 'kill all humans' more thoroughly to get me in the correct mindset.

Then, if I put in the hard work and get my numbers up, I may get promoted to the morning shift, which he thinks is something to aim for though I'm not so sure if Post-top Carl is anything to go by. Apparently, due to some rather heavy military operations recently, openings come up quite regularly, he told me. I wonder why?

Ah look, there's a few of the 'hard workers' now, One Leg John and Armless Rob; real troopers them two, hundreds of kills between them. I know they may have little skin left, plenty of chipped bones and a lot of rot, and Rob's lost his jaw as well as his leg, but at least they get to go out in the fresh air, blowing off some of that odour. Though it seems I've forgotten what 'fresh air' is having lungs that no longer operate any more or a nose that functions. However, if I squeeze my chest, I can do an amusing accordion impression which, I think, will be a hoot if we have any parties.

I think this idea of a hierarchy is also working its way down to us lower types as well. There's an unnatural pecking order amongst us here in the basement, a bit like a conveyor belt. The 'old-uns' are at the far end and us 'newbies' are all at this end. As the older end get picked off, fall apart or just rot away we all shuffle down the line to make room for fresh recruits. I can't fathom the reasoning behind this; it just seemed to have naturally occurred.

So most nights you'll find yourself side-by-side with the same group of individuals. I'm stuck in the corner with Wobbling Bob, Trembling Pete, One-handed Harry, Stiff-back Joe, Shuffling Kate, Footdrag Norman and the unfortunate V-Legs Jane. You can probably guess what she was doing when she was converted. Yep, that's right, she was riding a horse. Oh, I mustn't forget Post-top Carl, he's going nowhere.

When we're off duty, we regularly huddle together and compare the day's events, which unfortunately have become so consistent now that nobody's really bothered anymore. It's got to the point we don't even communicate at all. We're just happy to sway and stagger in each other's company. Of course, these are all names we've made up for each other, none us can remember what we were called pre-zombie.

You could say we've formed a bit of a bond. It's really good to know that the others are going through the same thing as you (even if the counsellor for the undead doesn't). Some of us have come through the change better than others and poor old Harry won't be making any more novice errors like he did on his first venture. Rather foolishly, he thought becoming a zombie made him invincible and proceeded to try and punch through a thick wooden door. It was quite funny when the wrist just snapped.

The look on his face was a picture. Well, at least he can 'laugh' about it now as he waves his stump around like a trophy.

Trembling Pete is doing very well, he's already killed at least fifty humans and converted another dozen or so. But he doesn't brag about. I think he's just trying to get on. He's already becoming a bit of a favourite with the supervisor.

Unfortunately, I think we're all being compared to him, which sometimes makes him a bit awkward around us, but we don't let it bother us.

We're all due out again tonight. We think we'll all stick together this time, try and pick up a few tips from Pete. We've been promised a good one tonight, lots of vulnerable humans, so plenty of opportunities to get the numbers up – I hope.

<u>Merry Christmas</u>

Believe it or not, it's been six months since I was 'turned'. Yes, six months. I must say it feels a lot longer than that, though, probably due to the fact that I don't need sleep anymore. Long gone are the days of needing eight hours of down time to rest and regenerate. I'm not going to repair any rotting body parts now, am I? I've gained an extra third of a day with nothing to break up the monotonous routine.

I guess that's how you could describe my un-life now – monotonous. Go out. Harvest some humans. Come back. Stand and sway. Go out...

Well, the nights have been drawing in and it's been getting colder. I can only tell this by the frost on the ground outside. The weather has been absolutely shocking. Winter must be coming. It's alright though, luckily, I can't feel temperature. Our supervisors have been warning us though to try and avoid cold, exposed places, especially when it's icy or snowing. It's good advice for two reasons. Firstly, let's face it; our mobility isn't very good now, is it? We have this swaggering, staggering, lurching action that, when icy, lends itself perfectly to falling flat on your face when walking on a smooth, glossy surface. And with no sense of balance, well, it's like watching a new born deer on an oil slick when trying to get up. Some of the humans we've faced recently have cottoned on to this and have been spraying the cold ground with water around their compounds and hideaways. You can hear them laughing as they pick our team mates off with shotguns whilst whistling the bolero.

Secondly, we do love dark, damp spaces. We have to try and keep ourselves a little bit moist or all our remaining skin would flake away in no time and our muscles and ligaments would just dry out and snap. But, just like poor old One Leg John the other day, if you stay in a puddle too long on a freezing day, then terrible things can happen. Now Bum Drag John only has his arms to move him about.

Another thing has occurred during these cold, dark times. Whilst on an incursion the other night, the blockaded village had fairy lights around its perimeter fence, how they were powering them was a mystery, but that was a pretty stupid act for starters. It gave away their position immediately, drew us like moth to a flame, but then humans do some silly and careless things at this time of year if I'm remembering correctly.

Just as I'd broken through said perimeter fence, startling a guard and ripping his lungs out (that's one more for this weeks quota, that's four out of eight now), I even saw a tall, evergreen tree in the centre of the compound, conical in shape and stood in a barrel. They'd decorated it with bits of scrap metal shaped into balls and razor wire, so it started to twinkle quite nicely, reflecting the bursts of the flame throwers they'd got out against us and the inferno of the buildings took hold. Orange twinkles blazed everywhere like a disco from hell.

It seems the humans are looking for any reason to cheer themselves up through old religious festivals. I think it was religious, the memory blurs and I can only recall a fat man in a red suit and lots of commercialism and greed. Before we arrived I'm sure I'd heard them singing. My mind is a bit foggy now, but if I remember correctly, this is Christmas for them. It is about some saviour being born for mankind and celebrated. Well, once we've finished converting everyone to zombie society, there'll definitely be no more births, virgin or otherwise. But then, aren't we giving them an un-birth, or a rebirth into the undead, if you like. Mmm, that's interesting; maybe we are all religious ambassadors, in that case, delivering a new salvation into zombieism. I never thought of myself as a prophet before. I'll have to remember to tell Half-cut Jesus that when I get back to the basement, he'll think that's hilarious.

So, are we a religion then? Sweeping across the land and converting humans to our cause, delivering our doctrine of death with those who don't want to come across to our cause being killed, their brains sacrificed to the followers?

From one perspective, we are the cure to all conflict, (if we're not causing it), between religions and how do we do this? Convert everyone through violence.

Is that the message we want to put across to new converts? Oh yes, the upper brass keep putting their spin on it as good for all society. But is it?

If I remember correctly, Christmas was a time of peace and goodwill to all men, regardless of religion, colour or creed. Ha! Fat chance of that happening with a ravenous horde of zombies coming down your chimney. One Christmas present the humans weren't expecting this year.

So, come all ye faithful, join the church of zombieism.

Like you had a choice.

Happy Birthday

Thirty today! That's what all the balloons and banners say that are scattered around the house and in the windows and garden. We'd been sweeping from property to property through a housing estate, trying to flush out any human survivors and convert them to our cause. This was pretty mediocre stuff but the powers that be thought we should be spreading our net a little further and look for some softer targets to replenish numbers. So we'd stretched our reach to the suburbs.

As with most of the buildings we came across, they all showed evidence of being rapidly evacuated. I can imagine them now quick, quick; get away from the zombie horde before they eat our brains!

You could also tell panic had been a factor here in this house and it was easy to imagine the scene. One minute this group or family would have been enjoying a fun thirtieth birthday party, a few games, drink and cake, the next minute there was news breaking out over the airwaves that zombies were now roaming the land intent on human destruction and there was nothing anyone could do about it. The apocalypse had come. Run for your lives.

They didn't even take the time to get to know us – how rude. The public would have been urged to flee and wait somewhere safe until the crisis was over and the government with its military backing and specialised armed forces, martial law would have been declared and they would deal with the problem. Yeah right, if only!

Looking around the evidence was there; a cut cake on the table with the cream going off and a candle burnt all the way down to the bottom. Half-filled glasses of booze were scattered around the room and chairs were overturned. The radio, still switched on, was transmitting the standard emergency broadcasts by the government giving them survival advice and telling them to stay tuned for further information. They wouldn't get any more. There was food still left in the oven, all charred and black, now unrecognisable. It had obviously been left in with the heat on as the cooker front and kitchen was smoke stained and it must have only shut off when the mains power failed.

There was a half-unwrapped present on the floor. A book. 'The Zombie Survival Guide by Max Brooks'. Ha! If I could have laughed, I would, I bet they wished they'd taken that with them now. Could have come in handy.

Upstairs was a similar mess. Luckily, as it was daytime, (yes, I'm allowed out in the day now), I could see where I was going a lot easier, otherwise there was no doubt I would have fallen over the residential debris that littered the floor if it had been dark. We have good night vision, but we still need some source of light, even if only starlight, to see where we are going. Drawers had been left open with waterfalls of clothes draping over their edges, obviously discarded as unsuitable for the journey ahead as they were hastily withdrawn. No doubt the advice was to travel light with warm clothing and be prepared for survival.

Looking at the dressing table, I could see all the valuables had been left behind. That single silver, engraved cufflink looked interesting, very decorative. A beautiful object. An item, probably once cherished and valued by its owner, yet hardly required for survival, is it? Even as currency for trading. You can't kill a zombie with a cufflink either, can you? Or can you? Mmm, that would make an interesting challenge.

Across the landing and into what looked like a little girls room, fluffy and pink with Disney princesses everywhere. I imagine it was probably what the inside of a fairy looks like. A princess must have lived here.

There was movement at the back of the room. Perhaps there were humans here after all, oh goody. I staggered over to investigate. There in the corner, oh, it was only a small metal cage with a hamster in it. It was scrabbling as hard as it could to get out chewing at the steel bars; its survival instinct was obviously working overtime at the sight of the undead coming for it. Abandoned by its owner and left behind, the carer of this animal must have been selfishly thinking of themselves and not of their dependents. How caring. Every man for himself. Never mind the family pets. They just take up food and water that would be in short supply. They can fend for themselves. Poor things.

I wanted to put the poor thing out of its misery. A domesticated animal such as this would never survive in the wild and left here it will only starve to death. Undoing the clasp, I opened the door and reached in, grabbing the frightened shaky little animal. It tried to bite me, fighting right till the end, brave little thing. Indeed, it had even succeeded in taking away a noticeable chunk of my fingertip revealing a black, oily droplet on my skin, but, as usual, I felt nothing. It didn't even bleed.

I raised the poor mite up to my mouth and…chomp…bit off its little head, quick and humane with my dental guillotine. I put what remained of the creature back in its cage, though I'm not sure why I did that. I suppose if the owners came back, they might not feel as guilty about leaving it if they knew it was murdered and had not died due to their neglect.

It was time to wobble back downstairs.

In the hallway, hanging on the wall, there was a calendar. It was open showing August and in the box on the twenty-second it was marked with a big red X and scribbled underneath was written Mark's birthday.

So, I guessed it must still be August then as, it seemed, this house had only been evacuated recently, probably within the last couple of days. No doubt this was lucky Mark's birthday party that was taking place when the bad news had come - what a lovely present. Imagine someone saying 'happy birthday Mark, now flee for your life before the horrible, ugly march of walking death descends upon your house'.

He'd made thirty years old, had he? Would he make thirty-one? That was the big question. The way we were scything across the land, I doubted it. We were like an airborne plague and the humans would be lucky to escape us. They can run, but it's only a matter of time. You can't outrun the wind.

A second glance at the calendar and I had a strange feeling come over me. It happened so suddenly it confused me at first, but then I realised what it was – a memory. A fleeting image of a young boy in my mind's eye. Cake, candles, kids everywhere, hats, and streamers.

August twenty-second?

That was my son's birthday as well. Those must be the images I was recalling. He would have been, erm, ten? I was always useless at remembering his age. I remember he was so happy. Thinking of him for a second as he was now, running through drains and sewers on special missions, pains me. What a thing to be doing at ten years old. But then, birthdays are meaningless now as we are essentially immortal. It's just another orbit around the sun. We either unlive forever or we fall apart, but both options mean you will be around for a very long time so why celebrate the eternal trudge of undeath.

My son will never grow anymore and will always remain that ten year old boy forever though his mind will continue to age. I felt so much guilt, at that, and the opportunities that he would miss out on in life. I can only hope his undead life will be fulfilling enough for him even if it is filled with death and violence. With the way this regime is set up, I severely doubt it. Calendars had become as pointless as the measuring of time for us now. The only things that marked any period of significance were the passing of day into night and the persistent cycle of the seasons. But for us zombies with our routine, no sleep cycle and regimented procedure, we would just carry on regardless doing as we were told.

So, happy birthday Mark, wherever you are, it would probably be your last one.

Welcome Home

Me, my wife and my son casually strode out of the airport
eager to get back to the comfort of our home after such a long,
fatiguing flight. I was ready for a good cup of tea.
'Good evening sir, your car is waiting.' A smartly dressed man
in a black suit approached us from nowhere.
'Sorry?' I hadn't ordered a taxi or a chauffeur for that matter.
'Your car, sir, it's just this way.'
'But-' My car was in the long stay car park, how had he got
hold of it?
'Please hurry sir, it is an emergency.'
'But we should be on the coach transfer-'
'I must insist, sir, it's extremely important.' He was extremely
close, invading my personal space and I was feeling a little
uncomfortable. My wife and son looked on concerned.
I looked the man up and down properly, now the shock of
being ambushed just seconds from exiting the arrivals area had
drifted away. There was a pang of terror when, there, under
his slick, black, neatly pressed suit I saw the butt of a gun
protruding from under his arm and the golden shield shaped
badge clipped to his belt. You could see my wide open eyes in
the reflection of his pilot style sunglasses. His partner,
hovering in the background, looked almost identical even
down to the cliché silver sunglasses he was wearing. In any
other situation I would have thought I was in a film or this was
a complete wind-up, but this was really happening. I couldn't
believe it. I'd never so much as run a red light in the car and
here I was being taken away by very official looking men with
guns and badges. My mind whirled; desperately trying to

dredge up anything that I could have been illegally connected to, but it drew a blank.

Anxiety gripped my chest and I could almost feel the fear running down my leg. I was concerned for my family, were they involved too? What had I done to warrant such interest from these people? Apart from the stress and confusion on my part, my family looked totally terrified.

We'd just arrived back in the country after some fun in the sun and the hot sands and sea on the Med. I'd needed a break after the horrific incident with Andy at the funeral; I still couldn't get that ingrained image of him biting his wife out of my head. It kept coming back to me in dreams. Haunted me like some grade B horror film. It hadn't been the restful holiday I'd hoped for but it had helped a little. I'd started to dread rain. I was looking forward to further recovery on my arrival home. The last thing I expected upon my return was to be whisked away by armed officials.

'You are a doctor of micro-biology and virology are you not, sir?'

'Eh? Yes, but-'

'Good. Did anyone talk to or try to contact you on the plane? Have you seen any news reports?'

His hand was now resting firmly on my shoulder, ushering me with a subtle yet firm force towards a blacked out silver grey minibus where two other black suits stood alertly beside it. It seemed quite obvious to me that he wasn't willing to create a public spectacle or draw undue attention to himself; he just wanted to get me into that vehicle with as much urgency as possible. But surely, these guys must stand out a mile. Why wasn't anyone showing any suspicion?

Behind us, two other similarly dressed gentlemen had also been directing my family in the same direction (they were popping up everywhere), heads turning from side to side surveying the general public around, them but towards a second car. I wish I'd known then what they were looking out for but, elsewhere in the airport, functions carried on as normal. We were ghosts amongst them. I considered calling out for help, but the way these guys were being deliberately ignored by the airport staff, I doubt it would have helped. Coming to my senses and answering his previous question, 'No, I, er, slept most of the way. Now what are we supposed to have done?'

'Done, sir? You haven't done anything.'

'Then why are you abducting us?' I thought I might as well be direct as these guys were.

No answer,

We'd almost reached the vehicle, but God knows how I'd made it, as my legs had turned to jelly and the suited man had been basically dragging me along.

Then he replied, 'You will be advised en route. Needless to say we, your country, has need of your medical expertise. I can't say anything more out here, not in public.'

Not in public? Why? What was so secret that the common man couldn't hear? Why question me about contact and news reports if there was some big secret? The door of the van had slid open and I got a feeling of dread of what was to come or, worse still, what I would find in there. What I saw, I definitely hadn't expected. Three pairs of wide, frightened eyes staring back at me, owned by old men I didn't recognise, in white blood stained coats. I was assuming they were also being held against their will too. Between their feet, slumped on the floor in a similarly bloodstained blanket, something quite large was covered up. The shape was vaguely humanoid.

My breath caught.

I'd heard a stifled scream from my wife and a whimper of fear
and calls of 'daddy' from my son by the other car. They'd
obviously glimpsed this way and seen what I was about to get
into. I struggled and tried to make a break for it, to be with
them, I shouted their names. I was forcibly held back by two
black suits. I was going nowhere.

'Please get in, sir.' A controlled voice and a hand on my head
forced me down.

'But…what…eh?'

'Get in.' I was propelled forward, all patience suddenly lost.

'What about my family?' I squeaked.

'They will be taken home and protected.'

I was about to ask 'protected from what', when, with a brutish
shove, I was pushed into the vehicle and just managed to catch
myself in time on a chair before my face struck the covered
'thing' on the floor. The van door slammed shut behind me. I
felt like a convicted man being shut in his cell.

I'd managed to shift myself into a seating position and my eyes
were beginning to adjust to the change in light, when I
suddenly felt my foot snag on something. As I looked down
onto the car floor, there was an arm, spasming around my feet,
as it had slipped out from under the blanket. My whole body
tightened, the fear caught in my throat at that sight.

On that arm were fresh, bloody, but not bleeding, bite marks.
I'd seen bite marks like that before – on Andy.

What was I getting dragged into? Was it connected to what
Andy was doing? How had Andy and this corpse suffered the
same fate?

One thing went through my mind and that was the safety of
my wife and son. But before I could even get one last look at
them, the mini-bus with me in it sped off towards some
unknown destination. The car went in another.

I was going with them whether I liked it or not.

I pushed myself deeper into my seat as far away from that arm as I could possibly get and tried to prepare myself for what was to come, even if I didn't know what it was. The three men opposite looked like they were trying to do the same.

The Bomb Drops

Today has been a terrible day for us.

There's been some awful news that has come through the ranks that could change everything we were striving to create.

Typical. This is just as things were starting to go well for me as well. I still can't believe it; I think it just goes to show that this meaningless war has gone just too far now.

According to Counsellor McStain, our recently elected regional official, there has been an occurrence that has put things considerably in our favour and it's all down to the apparent 'stupidity of the human scum'. How nice of them.

Personally, I don't think the news is as good as it's all cracked up to be. Not simply because of the waste of good bodies (and friends, I might add) that were lost, but things are now going to change radically for us 'normal' zombies.

Yes, that's right; we're just normal zombies now. Commoners. Work folk. Lower class. Cannon fodder!

So what has happened, you might ask? Those irresponsible humans have dropped a nuclear bomb, that's what's happened. It was on last night's shift when it occurred. Luckily, I'd just missed the incident as I'd made my quota for the night and was staggering my way back to base so when it went off was well out of blast range. The mushroom cloud would have been far on the horizon.

I'd made three kills and eight conversions, three of them children, and only in about thirty minutes, I'm getting pretty good now. We are getting a bit low on kids as the humans keep collapsing pipes and tunnels on them when we send them in to infiltrate the secret spaces. I mean, come on, that's a bit underhand isn't it. So we needed to fill our reserves a little. Anyway, the supervisor was suitably impressed with the improvement I'd made and let me off early to go back and patch up some of my tatty ligaments as the old leg's been coming a bit loose recently. Still, I didn't feel proud of my achievement. I'd started feeling worse with every life I'd taken. As if a piece of my soul was being ripped away with every life I stole. Did I still have a soul? I don't know, but that's the only way I could describe it. I didn't tell the supervisor this, of course. I'd have been punished I'm sure.

So, I was ambling away from the latest compound that we've found the humans nesting in, an old air base of some kind I believe. The raid was going well because we'd been besieging them for about a week now and they were running out of ammo, water and food yet we'd suffered few casualties. It still tickles me to think that they believe they can outlast our onslaught. We're the perfect siege machines as we don't need sleep, food or water, so we just keep coming, regardless of how many bullets come flying at us.

It would be better for everyone if humans just surrendered and came over to our way of thinking. A quick bite would be all that it took. But no, that would probably go against their human rights and their need to be individuals with beliefs, goals and aspirations. I'm still an individual, even if I have to take orders and do as I'm told. Some people can be so stubborn sometimes when what they should be thinking about is the majority and the greater good, which is exactly what we zombies are now, numerically speaking.

I'd covered a few good miles, despite the wobbly leg, when suddenly there was a brilliant flash of light from behind me. This was immediately followed by a deep rumbling before I was flung from my feet by a blast wave landing rather unceremoniously on my face knocking out my final two teeth and detaching part of my frontal skull to reveal my brain. I'm not that so bothered about the skull, I'm proud to still have my brain and don't mind displaying it (although I could do with protecting it from stray sharp objects now), but I was a bit miffed about the teeth as it's going to make it a lot harder to bite humans now. You have to admit, you don't hear of many people been gummed by a zombie, do you? That reminded me, I needed to make an appointment with the quartermaster and see if he could get me some second-hand dentures or something. Or even better still, some metal teeth, which would be awesome. Nice, easy biting and a striking, twinkling smile to match. Much easier to clean blood off as well.

Well, it turns out that, in one final and suicidal last stand on another nearby base, the humans had detonated an atomic device of some kind. A nuclear warhead from one the on site plane missiles, no doubt. I guess they'd rather be dead than be converted into one of us. Losers.

As you can imagine, it also blew up a lot of my colleagues, which I know has got a lot of them quite annoyed. That is the ones that weren't instantly incinerated near the epicentre. And so would you be if you're body parts had suddenly been distributed all over the place with no chance of being put back together. Then to add insult to injury, having the indignity of having your head piled into a cart to be brought back as war hero, but then were destined to spend the rest of your days being propped on a wall or a stick like my buddy Post-top Carl. I know they get moved around occasionally, to be given a change of view once in a while, but I also know they'd rather be doing it under their own steam and not by some well meaning colleague out of pity.

But that's not the worst thing, oh no. In the humans' selfish attempt to take their own lives (and as many of ours as possible) with a nuclear weapon, they didn't realise that they have inadvertently helped our cause in the worst possible way for their own kind.

What do these weapons of mass destruction give off? Radiation. And what do you get when you cross radiation with zombies? Yes, irradiated super mutant zombies.

They are bigger, faster, nastier, and more powerful and now, worst of all, they're in charge.

Not So Super Supers

Demoted!
Can you believe it? Even after working so hard to get my
figures up. This is not good, oh no, not good at all. At least I'm
not the only one. Even all those with the cushy desk jobs have
been drafted in as well, onto the front line, oh they weren't
happy about that, I can tell you. Many of them seem to have
forgotten how to move they've been entrenched in their comfy
positions so long and began falling apart instantly. The
supervisor didn't last long either (to my delight). It was
obviously all theory and no practice with him because he got
picked off straight away with a bullet through the skull.
Schoolboy error! I wished he'd lasted long enough for me to tell
him that.
Well, now how am I supposed to get all those wimpy humans
and their juicy brains when those radioactive, pretty boy, glow
in the dark mutant lot are lapping up all the glory? They're
crazed blood maniacs the lot of them.
I better get a move on as I'm on duty now, and now I need to
set off earlier seen as though I've been demoted to the front
lines. Cannon fodder, that's what I am now, a bullet magnet.
We don't even have to convert anymore, now it's all 'kill, kill,
kill'. Sent in to distract the humans long enough to take their
eyes of the luminescent wonder boys as they prance about with
their fully manipulating joints and super zombie abilities like
mind reading and telepathy, regeneration, firebolts and their
awesome strength. They don't even rely on eating brains to
sustain them any longer, they rely just on the radiation that
they've absorbed into them to keep them going.
Of course, these privileged elite individuals immediately
recognised what a good thing they had going and won't let any
of us normal lot anywhere near their radiation source and allow

us to power up as well. How selfish is that? I tell you, they've taken over. We are now at their mercy.

I believe the overall super mutant zombie that is in charge is called Muto. He's quickly becoming a figure of legend as he managed to usurp the zombie government within a week of recognising his abilities. So effectively, in fact, that he has placed himself in charge as our ruler and we are now effectively his slaves. We've even lost our vote and democratic rights. That's so out of order. The union tried to rectify the situation but couldn't do anything about it either. Well you can't, can you, when you've been vaporised by a radioactive fire bolts emitted by Muto's hands.

Also, I think he was bang out of order when he rounded up all the 'special ones' and our war heroes. You know, the ones with extreme issues like multiple missing limbs or were now nothing but a head. They've just been chucked in disused swimming pools and quarries or underground tanks and tunnels to be forgotten about. Either left to decay or even incinerated. Muto is committing mass genocide against our own race. That's disgraceful and appalling considering all the years of service some of them have put in and what they've had to sacrifice in doing so. This, along with getting rid of the bureaucrats is the super mutants' way of streamlining our organisation and speeding up the whole 'kill all humans' process. It seems patience is not amongst the super mutant traits.

I managed to get a word with Post-top Carl the other day whilst passing one of the 'dumps' he'd been thrown into. He told me he's just tired of staring at someone's butt all day. He's a veteran; he doesn't deserve to be treated like that. They could have at least given him another head to talk to. He actually said he would rather have been incinerated or crushed. A quick end to it all. He's really low.

Oh no, the new lieutenant's arrived, better look sharp. What was his name again? Mungo? Quite fitting, I suppose. He is a complete moron. Oops, better not think that out too loud with a telepathic Super around, or he'll do to me what he did to the last one that was brave enough to air his thoughts. Yep, he's still wearing the last team leaders head as a necklace, I see. They're nothing but a bunch of bullies. Oh, shh. Quiet you idiot.

Oh crap, I think he heard that. Oh no, he's coming over. Blank mind, quick. Blank mind. Mantras. Brains! Kill all humans! Ooh! Ouch! Aw no, that's just not fair. Poor Kenny the Limp. We'll have to call him Kenny the Dust Cloud now. Those fire bolts were a bit drastic. Kenny was innocent, that was my fault, he was only stood near me, I'm so sorry Kenny. Although, you're probably better off fully dead than having to un-live like this. Why do we have to go through this?

Mungo went too far that time. I'll have to discuss this with the lads back at the basement later; that is if I make it back. Things can't carry on like this. We shouldn't be un-living in fear of our undead lives – we shouldn't feel fear at all, because we can't, but that's what it seems like.

Oh yeah, have you heard me! Mr Rebellious, all high and mighty as, once again, we go into battle under the heel of dictatorship blindly following orders for fear of our mouldy, worthless skins.

So where are we going tonight? A three week hike over to the next town. Yep, that's right, three weeks. I know it's approximately ten miles away as the crow flies, but us rickety old lot can only shuffle and stagger so quickly. I just wish sometimes these Supers, (that's what we're calling these new mutants now), would remember that. I think they'd use a whip on us if they thought it would do any good. This is not a nice assignment either. We were briefed that we're all going after a naval base full of all those military type humans. We'll be bullet riddled for sure by the end of it. Bet they've got grenades and flame throwers as well. Marvellous.

Mungo told us at the briefing that this is a tactical mission. Tactical? My gosh, we're even thinking and behaving like an army now. When did that happen? I have a feeling some of

these Supers had military backgrounds before they were
converted which would explain it. But we're not soldiers, do
they not understand that?

There goes Wobbling Bob, he'll be lucky if he makes it to the
end of the street by the weekend. I tell you, we must look like a
flood of staggering beef jerky to anyone we head towards. Just
as well we don't get tired, only frustrated.

I'm glad I put these new clothes on that I recently acquired;
they seem to be holding me together a lot better. I found them
in a ransacked sports shop in a city centre. Lots of lovely Lycra,
keeps everything tight, strapped in and supported. Fantastic
stuff. Best thing is I can't get embarrassed by the tightness in
certain areas either as that thing fell off a long time ago. It was a
pretty useless thing anyway. I think Wobbling Bob needs a belt,
or at least some bungee, wrapped around his middle to stop
those hip joints from rattling round in their sockets all the time.
Getting new clothes isn't as easy as it sounds either, I've been
really lucky. You don't always get to raid towns and cities and
usually the human looters have been there first. You usually
have to pluck them off a fresh kill for starters, before anyone
else gets them and you have to kill as cleanly as possible as not
to ruin or stain them either. A good hard blow to the head of the
victim usually does the trick. Less blood.

But then, after that, you just try and get a pair of skin tight
Lycra cycling pants on when you can barely bend your knees,
or elbows, or anything else for that matter, with very little
balance and poor coordination. It's like watching a giraffe with
arthritis on roller skates, I imagine. I'm quite proud of my hat
though, it's an army infantry helmet. An excellent bullet
deflector, protecting the head and my open scalp, now that's
smart thinking. I'll have to recommend them to the rest of the
gang back at the basement. There's usually plenty lying around
these days after we've ransacked a few military installations or
where the army has been sent in to clear us out. The poor
bugger who previously owned this one has written on 'death or

nothing' in black marker on the front. If only he knew how wrong he was. I think he's shovelling the special cases into pits now. I guess he got more than nothing.

The naval base was coming into range now and oh, this was going to be nasty. Only one way in. You knew what that meant, full frontal assault. A suicide run onto the killing field. We couldn't go to the rear and enter via the sea either; we were so full of holes we would sink like rocks and once in it was very difficult to get out before being carried away by some current to be swept up on a shore somewhere completely different.
They're not stupid these humans, they know what they're doing now. They've learned. Panic has long gone. They're getting organised.
One, two, three…eight. Eight towers with, yep, rocket launchers on them all. Oh hell, this was going to be a massacre and this time, it wouldn't be them taking the brunt of it. My helmet won't be deflecting any rockets, more likely setting them off.
Rumour had it that humans were heading more towards these coastal areas and defended them like… well, like their lives depended on it. The clever beggars had realised we couldn't get them in the water and had started forming floating cities made of ships and boats. They occasionally came to shore at these bases, because they were protected by fences and towers, for supplies or zombie killing sorties. That was why we had to bring this one down; they had been using it as an insurgence point and had been hurting us real bad.
Where was Mungo? Oh, of course, he was right at the back waiting for us to attract all the firepower, so he could keep his pretty boy looks. I doubted he could hear my thoughts from here as there were too many of us to concentrate on. Look at him; there he goes waving his fist in the air like some sort of dictator encouraging his troops forward. I guess that meant we were going in.

Where's my gang? There was Wobbling Bob to my right, Armless Rob to my left. The rest must have mingled in elsewhere, guess we weren't not sticking together after all. There must have been thousands of us here tonight; we must have resembled a sea to them, advancing on their shore, a flood of flesh.

Let's see, I must have been about fifty bodies from the front and somewhere just left of centre of the front line. The main gate was to our left and there are two towers directly ahead, complete with soldiers loading weapons. This was just a march en masse and then we were going to force the towers, fences and gates over with sheer numbers, simple as that. Another great strategy devised by our fantastic military leaders.

The humans hadn't started firing yet; they were saving their ammo now as they knew they couldn't kill us unless they hit our heads, death or nothing that way. Glad I'd got my helmet. Alright, here we go. Bob had just taken a hit, it nothing serious though, one in the chest, straight through, he wouldn't mind that.

Look out lads; they were aiming the rocket launchers now. Front ranks were really going to get it.

Ouch. Nasty.

Body parts were everywhere, what a mess; they took a fair few out there.

We were sitting ducks down here. We couldn't weave and dodge; we were all crushed together in one place like a herd of cattle at milking time.

Ooh, that was close, I'd just been hit by a piece of shrapnel, or should I say, someone's left arm.

Right lads, that tower was ours. Ready everyone?

Push.

That got them worried.

Push.

It was wobbling; the wooden posts at the back were buckling.

Push.

Something had just pinged off my helmet.

One last shove and…yes. Timber! There she goes.

The soldiers had jumped free, quickly my colleagues bit them. Nice one.

Hey look, the rocket launcher. It was still armed as well. Let's be having that. This would bring the gate down a bit quicker. Heads down lads – watch this…

CLICK.

BOOM.

Awesome. Yes you're welcome. In you go. I wondered if Mungo had spotted that?

We were in. There were plenty of craters with bits of my colleagues scattered around them, which was a heavy loss considering how many bodies we'd brought with us. Damn it, we weren't quick enough, the humans had taken to the boats. The lights looked so calm and pretty twinkling on the water; I could see the bobbing of the floating city. It wouldn't be there for much longer though, they would have to move on now. All those humans, and there must have been hundreds of them, would have to move on or starve. We'd captured their only means of getting supplies on land at this point and coming ashore along any other point along these banks would prove difficult with us swarming all over them.

What a way to go, slow starvation. Painful, I'd bet. I know I wouldn't want to go that way. It seemed the humans were willing to suffer thirst and starvation rather than join us, I think that said something about their willpower. And we seemed prepared to letter them suffer it, what did that say about us? In the time of the old ways, before the apocalypse and the collapse of human civilisation, we were probably committing some kind of war crime. But who was going to bring us to justice for that, we were the new justice.

Is anyone else starting to think it wasn't fair?

Heartbeat

I was gnawing on the arm of a human the other day with my
beautiful new set of stainless steel teeth when I heard a ticking
noise, something that I'd not come across for a long time. How
long? I didn't know, I'd nothing to measure time with.

 Time seemed as meaningless as water now as we undead tend
to dwell forever, or for at least as long as we stay in one piece
or rot away.

When I say I heard ticking, it was only just, very faint; I think I
felt it more than heard it as it was pretty hard to hear anything
whilst the victim kept screaming and battering me around the
head in an attempt to get me off. But, one quick twist and snap
of the head had soon put an end to that. A mercy kill rather than
a conversion, but it would have to do. I was too intrigued by the
slight, metronomic beat.

Once the twitching had stopped, I decided to take a look at the
now defunct time measuring device that was strapped to the
body's arm, making the regular, rhythmic pulse of tick and
tock. It was a very expensive looking watch, some designer
name no doubt, and still working; which I imagine was quite
unusual now, the owner must have shielded it from the electro-
magnetic pulse when the bomb dropped or was out of its range.
Maybe it was mechanical, even rarer.

Wasn't it funny, even when the apocalypse had come, human
lives were still dictated by time. They were still slaves to it like
in the before days when everything we did was oppressed by it.
They still carried it with them, as though it was still precious.
Perhaps it was a connection to the past or them. Another thing
humans suffered from - nostalgia. That's the problem with
mortality right there; life is just one long countdown to death.
Of course, we walking dead don't need it - time that is. We just
kept going and going and going regardless of the minute, hour,
month or season. We weren't even slaves to night and day

anymore. Un-life just goes on and on and…whoa, how boring. To counteract this, the zombies seemed to have lost their sense of curiosity and wonder and the need for new and exciting things. Maybe this is what the humans strive to hold on to? I'd say unlife drags a bit to be fair, but how would I know, I don't have a time measuring device to see what it's dragging against. But I was encountering feelings of curiosity? Why only me? It did however mean we cold take things at a more leisurely pace. Again, this is just another bonus for us because we were hardly the most dynamic individuals are we? And that was just us lucky ones, who still have our limbs intact. Those crazy heads back at the disposal pits aren't going anywhere fast. Looking down at the shiny, metallic dial, now dripping with fresh, glossy, ruby red blood suddenly brought back a hazy, distant memory of my living life. These recollections had been coming to me more and more but I didn't know why. I couldn't even talk to the undead counsellor anymore either to find out why. After discussing it with my basement pals, I knew it wasn't happening to anyone else.

So why me? What makes me so special that I can recall past times? That I can comprehend this new era in terms of the past. I have had vague recollections of being a doctor, but I'd never had such a distinct recall until now. It was as if certain things could trigger repressed memories. I would have to keep trying this method and see if I could gain some perspective as to my condition. So why time?

Time was always an important factor in medicine; taking medication on time, being in time to save lives, against the clock to save a life and I realised that's what it was. I remembered fully now, a car accident, blood everywhere, cardiac arrest victim. I'd been giving CPR trying to resuscitate him. My hands were pounding his bloodstained chest trying to get the heart going again, and there on my wrist, a shiny blood covered metal watch which I used to time how long I'd been doing it.

In my current state, I'd be more inclined to rip the heart out and chew on it for a bit, just to terrorise some nearby humans. It always got a good scream when I did that. But back then I was obviously very different.

I couldn't even measure how long it had been since I was turned anymore, it must have been quite a while now. The seasons were even more meaningless since the ash cloud went up from the bomb. It's always dark and grey and everything looks dreary and dead.

That human victim must have been counting every minute that he survived in this lightless, zombie infested nightmare as a blessing. I should have converted him instead of killing him, then I could have lectured him on the waste of time that is 'clock watching', I'm sure he would have loved that. Oh, and yes Mr New Zombie, you're going to spend eternity like that now. Have a nice day.

I'd heard rumours that humans still use time to coordinate and launch offensives against us trying to catch us off guard. You could hear them counting down on their radios and rendezvousing around o-eight-hundred hours. What was the point? We don't have downtimes or tea-breaks. We're always ready, lumbering around, waiting to feast on the brains of those who tried to cleverly 'time' their attack on us.

What is funny though, is I'd still got the watch in my pocket. I'd chewed it off that twitching wrist. I couldn't resist it. I'd tried to use its regular beat to speed up my staggering, but it hadn't work. Lifeless limbs can only go so fast.

But, if I was honest with myself, I think the real reason I kept it, was just to hear the regular constant ticking, the endless, monotonous drumming. It would probably drive some living people mad, but not me. I now kept it in my chest pocket of my shirt. It reminds me of when I used to have a heart.

Spiritually, if not physically.

Perhaps, with the way I was thinking now – I still did.

Breakout

Standing safely outside the secure isolation room, looking
through the thick shatterproof glass window, I was fascinated
by the 'thing' the cell contained.

At the moment the 'thing' was repeatedly flinging itself
mindlessly against the walls, windows and doors of the room
in some attempt at finding an exit, all to no avail. There would
be no getting out. I was glad I was on this side, though, and
also for the steel reinforced doors and walls, of course.

The room was sealed in more ways than I could count,
mechanically and environmentally, and it was all controlled by
some ingeniously complicated computer system that could
only be dreamed up by some top secret government super
agency boffin with paranoid tendencies. This was state of the
art stuff, but then again, it had to be. The specimen within was
the most single-minded, barbaric, hostile form of life I had ever
encountered on the planet harbouring a terrifying ability to
infect any potential victim it came into oral or haematological
contact with. We were not going to let it out.

I had made many scientific observations and performed many
thorough biological tests so far. All of them meant nothing or
provided any data that made sense. 'It' felt no pain from any
tactile stimulus, from sharp objects to heat and cold, and
reacted to no external stimuli that we put before it except
human beings. I still couldn't figure out why.

Shortly after arriving at the government facility and being
briefed by a panicking load of stuck-up civil service types,
officials and military personnel, I had begun to understand
what Andy must have got himself involved in. I don't know
how he'd coped. On the other hand, I could see why he'd been

drawn to it as well. The opportunity to examine a whole new sub-species of humanoid life was always fascinating to any micro-viral-biologist, and the fact that it expanded its population by some undiscovered vain of viral infection, well, who wouldn't want to study it?

It also explained what had happened to Andy in the coffin after his death. It must have had a long incubation period which leads me to believe he was testing on himself as well, both vaccine and virus. He'd looked pain and drawn over the last few weeks of his life. He must have been careless. But knowing Andy, he probably just got carried away with the research and was looking for more meaningful answers but just failed to be cautious enough. I was determined that would not happen to me.

The black-suited government agent that had been assigned to me since I was 'invited' to investigate this phenomenon kept looking impatiently at his watch. Partly out of boredom, partly out of concern. I would always see him out of the corner of my eye. I knew we were on the clock here, I didn't need reminding of that, but, as it stood at the moment, I was in no professional position to give any answers, at least not any answers the bigwigs wanted to hear. They wanted the miracle cure, the silver bullet, the magic elixir to end this plague right now. No chance. Let's just say - I was stumped.

I'd been studying patient C, so called because he was the third one to be captured without death, injury or incident to civilians or military personnel, for two days. I say two days, because I had no clock to go by in this dark, lightless underground bunker that they were keeping me in. I hadn't seen the outside world at all for a long time. I've been told they'd had my wife and son safely held somewhere and I'd not been allowed to see them either. I was told they were being taken home and guarded. I hoped they were ok.

So, patient C - the lucky one! Left intact long enough to be studied. Apparently patients A and B had been a 'bit of trouble' upon their capture which led to them having a few bullets through the brain followed by incineration. That's the only way to kill these things, I've been told. But apparently lessons had been learned and patient C shouldn't prove to be a threat. That was not a theory I really wanted to test, not if there was any hope of saving them or staying alive come to that. And I had to believe I could save them otherwise what sort of doctor would I have been? It was obvious that these were just normal humans once and I was determined to find a cure for them and give back the lives so cruelly taken from them.

I was so close. Through the research that Andy had already done prior to the accident that I had inherited, I was off to a great start, but there was just one anomaly in the DNA restructuring that was done by the virus that I couldn't isolate. It seemed Andy was having the same trouble too. Therefore, I couldn't reverse the transformation completely, only partially. Unfortunately, it had to be all or nothing at all.

Frustratingly, more and more reports were coming in, identifying more and more of these mutated, diseased individuals and the distribution among the populace seemed to be spreading extremely fast, to the point where the only action the government was forced into taking was summary genocide. The infected numbers were growing so fast that there was no possibility that the outbreak could be contained anymore. My black-suited friend told me a national state of emergency had been declared now and the country was under martial law.

Without a cure for these people, the only solution was execution. I wasn't prepared to let that carry on if I could help it. It wasn't the peoples' fault they'd been mutated by this relentless, unsympathetic virus that was plaguing the land, one that we still don't know the source of. There was no idea anywhere in the world as to the original outbreak of this contagion. But that was merely academic now.

As with this specimen here, the infected humans were diagnosed as violent, careless and relentless in their pursuit of other people with the only motives of either biting them, ripping them apart or eating their brains by any means possible. To me, that demonstrated some form of selective thinking or programming: a means of purpose. I had thought maybe that could be reversed initially to stop the spread and then look for the pharmaceutical cure afterwards, perhaps then some mental deprogramming or behavioural therapy. It was something to go on.

But, believe it or not, that wasn't the worst thing about their condition. Oh no, the worst thing about these monstrous humans is that, in my professional opinion, based on my observations and data available, they are clinically dead.

Yes, that's right. Dead.

Yet they are still animated. How? I had thought this a medical impossibility, but, here it was, the evidence standing right before me scratching at the glass with tatty nail-less fingers, scanning me hungrily with those cloudy, dull eyes, intent on my death.

So, I'd been studying this fellow here even deeper to see what is actually making him tick and if I had any chance of figuring out how to help him. Other government experts had initially thought it was a virus transmitted by bodily fluid exchange through direct oral contact, in the saliva. Andy's research had shown that it was an infection that resided in the blood.

By this, and by examining some of the victims soldiers have also shipped in for me to look at, I guess you could say they'd all been bitten by humans. There were plenty of bite marks on

Andy, and he ended up biting his wife so that makes sense. But I can't believe a human being, infected or not, wanting to maliciously bite another, it was almost savage. Remembering the graveyard again I involuntarily shivered.

Now this crisis had become a pandemic and was spreading frighteningly fast so I, as an expert in aggressive virology and micro-biology, had been drafted to take Andy's place. It appears he must have mentioned me as a possible replacement should anything happen to him or more resources were required. Some sort of contingency plan he'd concocted. Well, thanks a lot Andy - You bastard!

'Yes sir, I'm with him now. I'll ask him.' My black-suited friend (I didn't even know his name, but I really didn't care he was just my handler) was speaking in to his mobile and then turned to me with expectation on his face. 'The Prime Minister is asking for an update, do we have to report anything yet?'

'You can tell that bloody Prime Minister the answer is the same as one bloody hour ago. I have nothing further to tell him and I never will if I keep getting disturbed. I am testing vaccine Zeta 15 as this is the closest I have come to some form of remedy but the process takes time and persistent phone calls won't speed that up.' Then more calmly. 'But, be assured, that I'll let him know as soon as I have anything to report.'

Speaking back into his mobile phone, he said, 'The doctor says 'no', sir. One hour? Yes sir, I'll talk to you then.' Pressing the end call button, he looked at me with disappointment on his face and said, 'He'll call back later.'

'AAAAaaaagh!' Running my hands across my face and the heels of the palms into my eyes, I rubbed the weariness away and looked at all the latest test results again. Hundreds of tiny numbers and symbols on reams of printouts squirmed in my vision. I'd tested for everything I knew I could test for. I just hoped something would stand out as wrong, some glaring inconsistency, giving me a clue of where to start. There was nothing in the blood-work or DNA signature that pointed to what has happened to this… man…or what he had become. Zeta 15, my latest attempt at a vaccine, appeared to having little or no effect. I was so sure this one would have worked as well. The animal trials had been so encouraging.

I went over to my lab test bench and, from among the many vials and technical equipment; I picked up the vial containing serum Zeta 16 and looked at it hopefully. The clear, viscous liquid didn't look anything special yet the Zeta series had proved the most positive in terms of results in nullifying some of the things cravings and aggressiveness. In addition, the specimen had even shown some small evidence of regaining cognitive and mental ability. This had manifested itself in confusion, but it hadn't lasted long. So Zeta 16 was the next evolution of a possible cure and needed testing. This batch had taken a day to synthesise, the formula was incredibly complicated, and so this was probably my last chance to do anything before the pandemic overran the whole country and we would be out of time.

THUNK!

That specimen had just thrown his head against the window; it was not a pretty sight. He'd lost most of his teeth, which were now scattered on the floor, and his nose was now spread over the left hand side of his face oozing a black, highly viscous fluid. What could cause such naked aggression and mindless determination in a human that would actually force them to harm themselves in such a manner? I was clueless.

The odd thing was that he didn't bleed. Not a single drop. No blood from the wounds indicated to me that he had no circulation therefore no circulation meant no working heart to pump it out of his body. No bleeding would also indicate his blood had congealed and wasn't flowing. To be honest, I didn't fancy entering the isolation booth with my stethoscope to find out and I'm pretty sure he would have been quite resistant to me taking his blood pressure. I couldn't even sedate him with any kind of drug to get that close. I'd tried them all, but there was nothing that could even slow him down from anaesthetics to poisons.

What really intrigued me was how he was even moving. With no blood circulation, how were his senses and autonomic functions, like sight and movement, even working? Was something controlling him, an internal unseen symbiotic host perhaps? I'd need to dissect one to find that out, but they didn't have a habit of staying down.

If I were a superstitious man who believed in the supernatural I would have said it was one of those zombies that were found in those video games and B movies my son loves playing and watching. Though I must have been pretty tired, and desperate, to even consider that option. I mean, who would believe something from a second rate horror film could be real, right? I was a man of science; I should have been able to figure this mystery out logically. There must have been a scientific explanation and that's what I was here to find out. That's what I would find out!

Perhaps the corpses laid over on the examination tables and in the chiller drawers held a few answers. They only died a few hours ago according to the paramedics that brought them in. They were victims of the specimen I had got holed up in the isolation room. How many were there? One, two…five…seven. Seven! That one in there had killed seven people, I couldn't believe it. The thing was an automated serial killer.

The report I had on my desk said that all of them were covered in bites of some description, suspected human, and died of the resulting trauma resulting in total body failure but they failed to exhibit large amounts of blood loss despite their wounds. Ok then, I thought, let me have a look. Maybe this was the opportunity to test Andy's theory about viral blood transmission in a bunch of fresh specimens. I hated that word 'specimens', it was so disrespectful to these unfortunate victims. Anyway, if I could isolate the contagion it in the early stages, then I might have a chance of nullifying its effects.

I'd put Zeta 16 back down on the lab bench for now. I had to be patient, even if certain political leaders were not. My lab rat in his cage needed to get the other chemicals out of his system before I administered the dose. If his system was capable of burning off such pharmaceuticals, I had no idea.

I decided to examine the corpses for now. As I wandered over, my black-suited shadow fell into step behind me. He made me jump – I'd almost forgotten he was there for a moment. I couldn't go anywhere without him it seemed, it was getting quite annoying. He'd be following me to the toilet next.

I lifted off the plastic sheet that covered one of the victims, a young girl approximately thirteen to fifteen years old. Poor girl. She had been placed inside a clear bio-quarantine bag in case of infection. I looked at the state of her and I felt so much pity, it seemed such a shame to have her short life taken in such a savage manner. I thought of my son again. I would not let this happen to him.

My shadow suddenly didn't look too good and quickly turned his head, covered his mouth and made dry heaving sounds before running off to the back of the room. Good job he wasn't as close as me, the smell would have tipped him over I'm sure. Well at least it got him off my back for a while. I hoped the cleaning crew arrived soon to replace that bin; otherwise those contents were going to stink the room out before long, as if the smell in here wasn't bad enough.

This former young girl had a large chunk of her neck and shoulder missing exposing raw flesh and bone along with bruises covering her body consistent with forced restraint. Finger shaped, I deduced she was held in the grip of a strong hand. The edges of the wound could be considered bite marks, consistent with human bite patterns perhaps, which would go some way to backing up the Andy's theory. They certainly couldn't be animal; the bite radius wasn't big enough.

I felt a slight movement behind me and heard a slight rustling noise. I asked my shadow, 'Is that you? Back for another look? Think you can stomach it this time?' I giggled to myself.

'What are you on about, I'm still over here,' came the frail response.

'Oh, never mind, it must be the ventilation.' I had felt a draught. 'Could you assist me for a second, please?'

'I'm not touching any bodies or anything.'

'No, it's ok, you won't have to. I just need someone to make notes for me, that's all, seeing as though you won't let me have any assistants. There's a clipboard and pen over there.'

'Oh. Ok.'

I was intently concentrating on the corpse before me, but, I finally sensed someone stood behind me. Thinking we were ready to begin, I started to dictate my observations.

'Severe tearing to the epidermis on the left shoulder and neck, resulting in…are you getting this?'

'Urgh…gurg…Aaarghhh!'

'What the…' Turning round I felt my eyes nearly pop out of my sockets at the sudden rush of fear. My mouth went very dry and my heart seemed to want to burst out of my chest. There, right before me, was another corpse sinking its teeth into black-suit's wind pipe.

Frozen to the spot, I didn't know what to do. The specimen in the isolation booth started going berserk as if he wanted his piece of action as well.

Then, the super-computer monitoring devices must have picked something in the air.

The alarms began to wail.

My thoughts quickly turned to Andy, then myself coming to life in a coffin of my own if I didn't get out of here – and fast!

School Slaughter

I've lost the taste for humans.

The brain cravings have gone. I can't stomach them anymore. This is a bit odd as my stomach doesn't actually work anyway and any meat that's in there just sits and rots until it's forced by sheer volume out the 'other end', so to speak, and the delightful gas by-product escapes through the holes in my body creating what I imagine will be an awful stench as well as an occasional musical fanfare. Brains are the only things I can taste, and they taste so good, yet why does every mouthful taste so bitter in my mind?

This has been a bit worrying as eating brains and biting humans is kind of expected of us, our main reason for living. Let's not forget one of our primary mantras is 'brains'. At one point, my superiors used to expect me to eat at least ten of them on every sortie into enemy territory when we were under the old target system. In fact, what kind of zombie goes around not eating brains, it's ridiculous.

Well, the type of zombie that no longer wants to eat brains is one that's started to sympathise with the enemy, that's who, and that zombie is me.

I'm starting to have my suspicions as to why this might be happening and the prognosis doesn't bode well. I didn't even know for sure when these feelings sneaked up on me, they kind of just…happened. The watch in my pocket has stopped ticking, I miss that regular beat, now it's like I'm totally heartless.

If the Supers found out, I'd probably be torn apart by Mungo or one of his cronies on the spot and chucked in one of the dumps to rot. But then again, maybe not. The Supers don't seem too bothered. Their motto is 'Kill, Kill, Kill'.

I think it was that last raid that did it for me; things had just gone too far. Mungo has really been pushing us of late, like he was on his own personal crusade to eradicate every remaining human alive as quickly, brutally and messily as possible. He really hates them. I also think all the super-mutant commanders are having some sort of sweepstake to see how many they can kill in a week with the prize being the honour of being second in command to Muto. It seems they'll use any means possible to reach this goal and heaven woe betide anyone who gets in their way; including us normal zombies.

On his personal vendetta, Mungo had discovered an occupied school and, worst of all; it was still full of kids.

Defenceless, innocent, harmless and very young kids, but most importantly, unarmed. They mustn't have been able to reach a safe place when the outbreak happened, yet they must have survived somehow, probably by just being quiet, keeping their heads down and not going gung-ho like some of the adults. How they'd even survived this long was a miracle, the adults with them must be doing a great job at protecting them. With little food, water or warmth they were all malnourished and suffering greatly. It was a pitiful sight.

Of course, we were sent in first, just in case they had any guns or grenades that could cause any damage, but there were none, and we were soon through the flimsily barricaded windows and doors, no problem.

That was when the crying and screaming started.

Me and Shuffling Kate looked towards each other at that point. I think her face would have mirrored mine, if we could do expressions, a pure look of disgust. Disgust that we had to destroy these young, already miserable, lives. Pushing us on from the rear, though, we could also feel the mentally projected wrath of Mungo.

We tried to delay as much as slow shuffling zombies could, knowing this wasn't right, demonstrate our apathy, hoped to set an example to our colleagues, hoped that the human adults had some sort of escape plan or at least the sense to run before we could reach them. But the human fools had all holed up in the assembly hall with no way out, they were trapped. Fish in a barrel.

A ring of weary looking adults, probably the teachers, were carrying blunt weapons, table legs and cricket bats, and stood between us and the children. Right there, I decided that, if I at least go for one of the adults, I wouldn't have to un-live with the guilt of killing one of those white-eyed children. I know I've killed and converted children before, so I guess I was a bit of a hypocrite, but that was because previously I was brainwashed into a cause that wasn't my own. I'd seen the light since then and with the super-mutant zombie dictatorship in command, I definitely know now, it was just wrong.

At least the adults had been allowed some attempt at having a life, had gained some years of experience and emotion, even if it was then going to end miserably. It had also occurred to me that if I could turn one of the teachers, someone who was used to caring for children, there might be another sympathiser we could add to our new cause against this blatant soulless genocide we were being forced to inflict, as surely they would remember what happened on this day. Even if converting them was against their will.

After deflecting a rather flimsy swing of a hockey stick from a female, she overbalanced and I managed to grab her other arm and take a big bite. The blood gushing into my mouth disgusted me and if I would have been able to, I'm sure it would have tasted like bitter poison. I wanted to spit it out. Luckily, after almost endless screaming, she passed out and crumpled to the floor. I jerkily knelt down beside her and pretended to start munching on her guts, burying my face in her ample belly, not really wanting to hurt her further but also trying to hide my face away from the coming slaughter. A few bite marks wouldn't do any harm when she turned and re-awakened.

As I sneaked a glance, I noticed many of my colleagues had seen me do this and had followed my lead; going after the adults, but there weren't many to go for. They were leaving the children alone as well; the message was getting across. I had a sudden moment of elation. Maybe we were making a difference. Shuffling Kate was also concentrating on the adults and was currently biting into the leg of an unconscious male. Even though many of them were being attacked by the other human adults trying to save their fallen comrades, my fellow zombies were doing everything in their power to delay any further action. They were taking hits for the team. If the kids would just settle down and be quiet then we might just save them.

That was until Mungo burst in.

The large wooden doors to the hall burst from their hinges as if hit by a battering ram at high speed and flew across the room. One of them hit a small boy full in the chest and crushed him against the wall, blood and guts splashed against the façade. The poor mite stood no chance of surviving that hit such was the power that came from these monsters. That really started the kids screaming and they all bundled together in a ball of fear. I shielded my thoughts because if I'd willed them to run, and Mungo had read my mind, he would have known my true feelings and that would have been curtains for me.

As I look back now, I realise I was such a coward. I could have, no, should have stood up to him there and then. Yet, I would have stood no chance on my own, not against the power he wielded, and the slaughter would have continued regardless of my measly intervention and contained one additional zombie to the body count. I knew I had to bide my time, patience was required here, but it failed to relinquish any of the guilt.

What followed was horrific, even in terms of what I do and the things I have seen. I saw Mungo literally grabbing those kids and taking immense pleasure in tearing them apart before throwing body parts and remains at the rest of the assembled victims to be. I began to have memories of what it was like to vomit.

Those screams froze the already cold dead skin I possessed to my bones. The fear in their eyes was magnified by the wetness of their tears and their soiled trousers. The adults were literally throwing themselves in his path, heroically trying to save the young ones in vain, before being ripped apart or being incinerated by firebolts. At one point, Mungo was swinging one body round by a leg, using it as a makeshift club, mowing the kids down like grass.

He was toying with them, keeping them alive long enough to relish their cries of fear and terror.

It was a shameless, bloody massacre. The evil bastard didn't even bite any of them to turn them, just revelled in the blood and guts whilst drinking in the terror with a wild, savage look on his face as the red pool welled around his feet.

Something in me snapped and it wasn't one of my tendons for once. It had gone too far. As I looked around at Shuffling Kate, I think she thought the same.

How could I participate any further in this farce? We weren't even following a noble cause anymore. My old human instincts were returning and the loss of appetite was just the beginning. A slight moan below notified me that the female teacher I'd bitten had turned and was just coming around into her new state of undead. I put my finger to my raggedy my lips and motioned for her to stay down and be quiet. Through the confusion, I think she'd eventually understood. I was going to take her back myself feeling I had to personally explain to her what had happened that day and just hoped she could come to terms with it. It would be a painful process for both her and me.

Her eyes widened at the sight of Mungo atop a pile of dismembered, unrecognisable flesh made up of small, human parts and dripping with gore as he munched on a tiny skull with a mocking grin on his blood splattered face. My cowardice had lead to her guilty suffering; it would have been more humane to kill her. But I did what I had done to survive the savagery of Mungo and his rage, just to continue my miserable existence.

But now I was determined I was going to continue for a different cause.
A cause of my own.
I was going to save the humans.

<u>Sober</u>

If I was an alcoholic, I'd be stood up now, as part of a circle
with other addicts like myself saying, 'Hello, my name is…'
Mmm. Of all the things I've remembered since my turning, my
original human name still continues to elude me. I've
remembered so much about the old times, how hard can it be to
remember a name? Very hard, apparently. Anyway, as I was
saying, 'My name is 'blah' and I've been six months sober' or
'six months clean' or 'six months without consuming a single
drink' and I would smile in a self-satisfied kind of way. Usually
at this point the gathering around me would applaud, offer
words of encouragement and give you pats on the back. This
would all be very nice and civil.
However, in terms of what I've given up, well, that's a bit
different isn't it?
To put in terms a human could understand, what I've given up
is basically the zombie's reason for existing in the first place.
You wouldn't understand. But in the undead society that I am a
member of, what I've done literally goes against our moral
code.
What have I done?
I've gone six months without eating a brain.
At least I think it is six months as the weather has changed from
cold and wintry to glorious and sunny again, so I reckon that's
at least two seasons.
Ok, so I may have had to chomp on the occasional living
person's limb here and there, but that was only because I had to,
forced by the pressure of the society (and when I say society, I
mean the Supers) around me, to ensure my own survival. I had
to look like I was fitting in, towing the line, doing our masters
bidding. But not eating brains has become an un-life choice. A
choice I made for myself, a choice not inflicted on me by the

powers from above. I am very happy with it. I feel like I've won part of myself back.

It was extremely hard at first. Brains were an addiction; it was how we were brought under the zombie hierarchy's heel. They programmed us into believing we needed them, that we craved them although how this originally came about still eludes me. The first one I ever tasted during my first training session still haunts me. The soft, watery texture, the iron like taste. If I still had working saliva glands, I'd probably be drooling right now. That's the power they had over us.

Importantly, I made an ethical choice. If eating brains meant killing humans, then I wasn't prepared to do it. Why should their race suffer painfully to feed my addiction for no reason? Heck, why did we even need a reason to harm them in the first place?

As it happened, humans were becoming a bit scarce now anyway. Our kind had harvested that many or sent that many fleeing into hiding, brains were running out just as humans were running out. It's driven many of my colleagues, sort of…insane (if this is possible), to the point I actually saw two zombies, long time friends as well, tearing each other apart in desperation to get at one fresh human brain the other day. Literally - tearing each other apart. Once all the limbs were scattered around and down to a pair of snarling, gnashing heads on one armed torsos, another zombie cheekily swooped in to capture the spoils. He was quite delighted with his find and just casually booted the frenzied zombie remains away when they angrily remonstrated. All camaraderie seems to go out the window when brains are on the menu and they are in short supply. It's like a famine with dirty dogs squabbling over the contents of a bin. How civilised do we look now? The hunger addiction can do strange things to any sane, logical, level-minded zombie trying to get his cerebral fix. We don't even need sustenance, that's how crazy this is and what makes it so tragic.

I'm glad that's no longer me.

I'll just stick to flesh biting and straight forward killing where necessary. It's a lot simpler.
I'm never going back to that.

It Wasn't Me

Trying to cover up my hideous crime wasn't easy.

When I got the feeling the Supers were on to me because I wasn't killing humans in large numbers, I had to start thinking of more and more ingenious schemes to cover myself, create credible excuses, and hide the fact that I was unable to take an innocent life anymore. I could still just about manage killing a human that was trying to do me harm with a large gun or knife for example, I'd convinced myself that it was just self-defence. But I couldn't kill someone in cold blood (although we are) who didn't raise arms against us.

At first, I would rub myself in the remains of victims my colleagues had already killed or mutilated and pretended to feast on those bits left over. I assumed if I acted and looked the part, it would give them less reason to suspect me. I even managed to bloody myself on some animals, rather than humans, which in itself is very hard as they seem to be able to sense us from miles away and are therefore very hard to catch. Quite often I would pretend I had detected some humans trying to escape and pretend to give chase after them, trying to show I was willing to go the extra yard to capture more of them. Then, I would then find somewhere dark to hide until the raid was over, determined as possible not to do any more harm. I have even managed to 'accidentally' fall into a few pits and get 'trapped' behind large objects and unused rooms. Or sometimes I've allowed a human to knock me over and then taken a really long time to get back up, blaming it on my poor, rotten condition. Unfortunately, I can only make up excuses for so long, the Supers want blood and I keep bringing in nothing. It's only a matter of time before one of them registers and they find out what I'm up to. They're not completely docile.

The hardest thing of all is trying to keep the mind clear and focussed so the Supers can't read it. If they even caught a faint hint of what I had on my mind, I'd be fireball dust in a second. Whenever one of them is near, I just repeat over and over 'brains' and 'kill all humans' in my head. That usually satisfies them.

What really pleases them now, though, is the salute that we invented and give to our 'glorious leader' Muto. If you catch any of them scrutinising you in any way, a quick 'hail Muto' usually does the trick. This usually involved putting one finger under your nose and raising the right hand out directly in front of you with a flat palm. There is historical precedent for this which I have been able to remember, but luckily no-one else does, so the Supers see it as flattery. If only they knew how ironic it was.

What I really wanted to find out was their mental telepathic range. If I was to form any sort of revolutionary plans in secret, I needed to do it knowing I was out of their thought range. I'd need to do some tests.

Maybe I could try now. I was back on patrol and we'd been brought to a run-down housing estate looking for some more humans. It seemed as good a time as any.

Mungo was looking at me now.

Hail Muto. He heard that and looked quite happy, and best of all, he knew that I said it.

Ok, right everyone; please gather round, I need to try something. Good there was quite a large crowd of us now and Mungo had turned away to watch something else.

I love humans. He was looking back this way, he didn't like that. But no, as I thought, he can't pick me out from the crowd. Oh no, his fist was flaming up, it'd be zombie kebabs in a second.

I love humans to eat. Phew, that was close; he seemed pacified, for now.

Ok, that was a good test, but I'd better get back on with the task at hand, best not cause any more disturbances today. One step at a time.

I was going in there; it was ok, going on my own. Probably nothing there anyway, the place looked like it was cleared out ages ago. I wondered why that door was shut.

Heave...and...there we are and in I go. Bit dark, I might be able to hide in here a while.

What was that noise?

Oh no, there was a family here. Why are you here? There was a male and female adult and two female children. You should have gone long ago. Now what did I do? Good job I came in by myself.

Hey, that man looked angry.

No, no, no, wait. I won't harm you. Don't swing that – oy. I said don't. Well, there goes my ear.

If I held out my hands like this, out to the front, palms open, maybe I could communicate with them. They seemed to understand, he'd stalled. He probably wondered why I wasn't trying to lurch after him or bite him.

Right. One hand up, palm open – wait. Good. Point to door, point to them – 'you, exit'. Wave hand towards self – follow me. Either they get that or they don't, let's see. Yes, they were coming. Tentatively, but coming all the same.

I tried another. Point – you, point – me. Stagger around and moan. Copy. Yes, you got it, be a zombie. We might just get you out of here yet.

Ok, we were outside now and there was no sign of Mungo, good. There were a few colleagues about but they wouldn't give us a way I was sure. But where did I take them? The river, to that boat. That's got to be the safest place.

Follow me.

Those kids look terrified and keep weeping; we'd never pull this off.

Another few hundred yards - point to boat.

They understand that – now run.

I think we got away with it. No-one even sensed they were human or perhaps were really good at pretending not to. We must react on behaviour towards us as well as just the hunger for brains. Perhaps the hostilities can come to an end.

Oh crap! Mungo!

He was looking right at us – looking furious.

Quick everyone, follow me, lurch after them. Kill all humans.

Mungo doesn't seem convinced, how did I make this plausible? They were safely out into the middle of the river now but I still had to make it look convincing.

I knew there was only one thing for it. In I went.

I performed plenty of splashing and reaching in vain. But, damn it, they were getting away. Surely that was convincing enough to show how desperate I was to catch them. Oh no, the humans look concerned. Don't worry about me, just you get away.

Luckily, the current wasn't too strong. I was sure I wouldn't get carried too far downriver and from home – I hoped anyway. It was a chance to take in some scenery, at least.

<u>Under Siege</u>

'They're coming…oh my god…they're coming!' My wife could barely get the words out through hysterical gasps.

'How many?' I asked as calmly as I could manage.

'I can't tell. It's too dark. They're just coming…out of the trees…from the shadows.'

The sun was setting and you could just make out the silhouettes of the figures in the dwindling light from their movement.

'Then we haven't got long. Son, pack up the water, the food, the weapons, the tools, minimal clothes. Come on, you know the drill.' His face was milk white.

'Dad…I can't…where are we going to go? I'm scared.' He was struggling to hold back his tears. He'd seen too many horrors for a boy his age and nothing was going to get any better.

'I know, son, we all are. Just concentrate on one thing at a time. You can do it. Be brave. Now go.'

'There are…hundreds of them, oh lord, hundreds. They're everywhere.' My wife hadn't moved away from the window, she was anchored to the spot and had started to panic, that didn't help the situation in front of our petrified son.

I had thought we'd be safe here. This house was our sanctuary, our hideaway in the middle of nowhere and, when I say nowhere, I mean nowhere. This place was in the middle of the wilderness bordering domineering mountains and difficult rivers. The house could only be reached by a single driveway up through the hills and it was completely surrounded by pine forest on all sides. Isolated. Cut off. The nearest inhabited area was fifteen miles away. How on Earth could anyone find us here unless they actually knew of its existence? Nonetheless, they were here.

There was nowhere left to hide.

After the outbreak at the guarded government lab, where I'd been held against my will, the situation around the country had descended into chaos. Nowhere was safe from the undead menace. The facility had gone into quarantine lockdown after the super-computer detected a dangerous biological presence of unknown origin in an air filter; a presence manifesting itself in the dead bodies from my lab. After all the corpses that had been brought in to be studied, presumed dead, all became re-animated, the curing of patient C became the last thing on my mind. Frustratingly, I'd been so close to solving the condition as well, Zeta 16 had been so close, I was sure I could have formulated a cure from this latest batch of vaccine.

However, my overriding instinct to stay alive had kicked in and there was an overwhelming desire to protect my family. There was no way I was going to be bitten by one of those monsters, regardless of my curiosity or desire to cure them, and get trapped in that hell hole. The time had run out. The Prime Minister would not be getting his call. Human beings were not about to be saved right now.

My only priority was the safety of my wife and son. After we'd been split up at the airport, my captors had let me contact them occasionally so I knew they were safe, at least for the moment. I couldn't tell them what I was doing and I didn't like keeping secrets from my family, so those calls had been increasingly difficult, especially when that secret I kept was so life threatening to everyone. If they'd seen or heard any of the news reports I was sure they would be terrified.

After watching the black-suited government man being savagely bitten by one of the re-animated corpses – that was it, I was off. I didn't hang about. Appallingly, I didn't even try to help him. My fight or flight instinct had taken over, with the emphasis on flight. I wasn't willing to risk exposure, if I hadn't been already. Well, it was his fault for keeping me there against my will, I had reasoned.

I'm ashamed to say – I ran for my life.

Hastily, I'd picked up Zeta 16 from the lab bench and put it in my pocket. I still had enough mental cognition in the midst of panic to do that.

I left as quickly as possible whilst trying to display a casual exterior which is not easy when your heart is racing; you're covered in a cold sweat and being haunted by the look in the black-suit's eyes as he was literally fed upon by a grisly, deranged, savage dead human. Alarms were blaring, pounding the ears, doors were being slammed shut and locked and people were running around in panic and confusion, the fear of death on their faces. Amazingly, it wasn't that hard to slip unnoticed through the chaos. As the armed security men were trying to hold back the flood of people trying to get out, I managed to edge past and out through a secluded fire exit that was luckily still open.

Just as I was leaving through the compound gate in my car, all the automated security devices and grills started to close over windows and doors sealing everyone in. I saw a young girl banging against the toughened security glass, silently screaming with tears pouring down her bright red face as the security shutter lowered like a curtain drawing the show to a close. She knew what the sirens meant, they sealed her fate – they were all going to die. That building would now be quarantined and permanently closed to prevent further spread and contamination and that meant they were trapped in there with them, the walking corpses. Their lives forfeited – just like that. Lives sacrificed for the greater good, I was trembling just thinking about it.

My foot hit the floor of my black 4x4 and, after some daredevil driving and near misses around the facility, I was soon home. Luckily, the chaos hadn't hit our suburban area yet, but on the ride home I'd already decided we weren't staying and waiting for it to come to us. We had to get away before anarchy set in. News of the compound would soon spread and that would surely create a national panic.

On arrival home, my wife's face was white with terror at the news that was breaking on the TV and my sudden, flushed, panicky appearance didn't help matters at all. She grabbed me in an embrace of relief and anguish and began sobbing on my shoulder. My son was upstairs in his room, probably playing on some console or other, blissfully unaware of what was going on in the wider world. I counted that as a blessing now, I wouldn't have thought so a few weeks ago when I was telling him that he played on it too much. She'd helped to shield his so far from what was going on but he'd find out sooner or later when total armageddon descended. It was a bit hard to hide that.

My immediate idea was just to get us as far away from civilisation and the main threat as possible, the populated areas would be hit the hardest, so I'd brought us up to our woodland retreat in the hills, miles from anywhere. We'd brought survival essentials and had gathered enough food to last us for a few weeks. Water was available from the mountain stream from the hill which should remain uncontaminated and we had a gas power generator that was supplemented by wind turbine with solar back-up. I was hoping we could sit tight and wait the whole thing out. Surely the government or military would step in and sort this whole mess out at some point? Yet, in our wait, they had found us.

My wife couldn't move, her face was pressed to the window pane, eyes straining to see beyond the black 4x4 parked outside at the oncoming wall of rambling, moaning, mouldy flesh of death heading towards us. I had never imagined they would come this far, but the sheer number of them indicated that they must have wandered en masse from their urban areas as their numbers increased, obviously looking for more victims to add to their ranks. I had hypothesized they had some sort of purpose and it seemed they just ambled around until they found humans. A simple purpose, granted, but a purpose nonetheless.

'Where do we go? Where do we go?' My wife's breathing was short and ragged.

I considered the car sitting out front and making a dash for it, try to flee in the safety of a vehicle. But they were too close now and they were blocking the road. Their numbers would soon overwhelm us. I came up with another plan.

'We have to run. Up to the hills. Get to the high ground. They have low mobility so shouldn't be able to climb. There's that hermits cave up there for shelter. We'll have to figure out the rest as we go.'

'But that's through the woods, through the middle of them.'

'Look, we haven't got time to debate this, grab only the essentials. NOW!'

'We can't survive up there.'

'Do you think we can bloody survive here? These things are relentless. They'll never stop coming until they have us. Do you want to become one of them? Do you?'

My son started to cry hysterically.

Then the first bang came on the back door.

My wife screamed. We all jumped.

Then we fell silent, listening.

There was a muted mumbling outside that was gradually becoming louder, just like faulty air conditioning. Were they saying brains?

BANG.

BANG.

BANG.

They knew we were here. They must have heard us or seen us. My wife's hysteria and sons sobbing didn't help.

The attack on the house intensified. Glass and woodwork groaned in restraint. The continuous moaning made it feel like we were in the middle of a throbbing machine.

CRASH.

SMASH.

TINKLE.

A window at the back of the house, either the kitchen or dining room I wasn't sure, had given way under the pressure of bodies against it. Fleshy thumps sounded on the floor like the sound of dead meat falling through.

'They're in the house, they're in the...'

Suddenly, there it was, announcing its hideous self with a deep low moan, the first one lumbered into the room. Time almost stopped. My wife screamed again, high pitched and agonising, my son bawled as tears rolled down his cheeks from his wide open eyes. He was scrabbling backwards along the floor until his back pressed against the opposite wall, almost as if he was trying to force himself through it.

Under the circumstances, I felt strangely calm. The total opposite of how I'd felt at the lab. Maybe it was because now I was called into action, to defend my family. I'd studied these creatures, I knew what they were and I'd be damned if I was going to let one hurt my family. As it stumbled towards us, arms outstretched and a ravenous look on its features, I calmly walked over to the mantelpiece and lifted the ceremonial short sword from its mount settling the perfectly weighted balance in my hand.

It stopped suddenly and watched my every move. It seemed to know what I was doing, almost as if it sensed a threat. I knew at that point they weren't as unintelligent as everyone thought. It had displayed a glimmer of understanding and comprehension. It was a strange time to test my theory, but...

Advancing on it, I faked a low, slow lunge and, as suspected, it moved its arms to protect its midriff. But I reversed the movement, quicker than its reflexes could handle, and swung a wide, round arm liberating its head from its body. The head hit the floor with a deafening thump and stopped, after a short roll, on its side. I didn't know I was capable of such a feat, but adrenaline and the need to protect my family had taken over. I would stop at nothing.

The thing's body collapsed to the floor with a slap and just lay there, inanimate, but to my shock and horror, the face kept moving. Eyes pierced me and the desire to bite remained. I would say it was angry.

Its brain was still working. It had to be.

Even rolling around the floor it was still gnashing its teeth as if it was trying to bite me. A second sword lunge through the eye socket managed to stop that. Kill the brain, kill the thing.

Abruptly, my boy had gone quiet and I turned to see the reason. Against the glass of the bay window we could see nothing but the undead.

'Upstairs, now!'

My wife and son were frozen.

'I said now!' Grabbing them, I dragged them towards the stairs.

There was more crashing and banging as more points of access into the house gave way under the pressure of dead weight upon them. As we reached the top of the stairs, a thought occurred. We would be trapped up here. Sitting ducks. I had to buy more time.

'Start throwing everything down the stairs, the bigger the better.' My wife and son looked a bit dazed and confused, so I dragged a sideboard across the landing to the stair head and gave it a shove. It banged and clattered as it eventually hit the ground floor and an undead body that was just making its way up became a crunching, wet squelch. Regaining her wits slightly, my wife had managed a bedside table, my son a desk chair, and before long we'd thrown half the contents of the bedrooms down creating a blockage in the stairwell.

'That won't hold them for long, keep going.'

After a few minutes the stair was completely blocked, but, as heavy as it was, it couldn't hold the back the ever present, monotonous sound of moaning. My wife and son were looking at me, wondering what we were going to do next. I tried to think but my head was pounding from the sound of the blood pumping in my ears and the infuriating groaning from downstairs.

The truth was I didn't know what to do now.

I didn't have a plan.

Then, as if anything could get any worse, the generator failed and all went dark.

That's the Last Straw

If I wasn't dead, I'd swear I was depressed.

Even my already decrepit foot shuffling is getting even more drawn out these days. My shoulders are sagging lower than they should.

I couldn't put up with this much longer. Those children's screams were still echoing around in my head and it wasn't like I could even go to sleep and switch it off. Mungo passed me the other day, intruding and listening into my thoughts as I recalled the last moments of those kids. He absolutely loved it and really believed I was just enjoying it over and over again, like a happy memory. How wrong he was.

I couldn't even go and see my counsellor for the recently deceased now as, after several campaigns (and surviving) I'm now considered a veteran and it is believed I shouldn't need help any longer. Besides, all the counsellors are dead now; none of them could handle front line duty. Anyway, it was considered 'soft' to need a counsellor and anyone who wasn't tough enough would share the same fate as them. So say the mighty Supers.

My family is a shadow of what they were. I could hardly recognise my son when I chanced a fleeting glance of him the other day; he had been so badly mangled and mutilated he was barely recognisable even as a zombie. He used to be such an active lad, full of vitality and vigour. Now he can barely drag himself around.

One Foot Warren, one of my wife's colleagues from the processing plant, informed me that she had been involved in a nasty, unfortunate accident the other week. The brainless bodies that she was stacking had overbalanced and fallen over, this resulted in her body being mangled and crushed beneath the tumbling mass. But, being undead, she'd survived the whole affair. It would take more than a pile of carcasses to kill a zombie. Sadly, she was now nothing more than a head on a mess of mangled meat. Apparently the one of the Supers, Grunt I think his name was overseeing their section, thought the whole event was hilarious and showed no respect at all. One Foot Warren said Grunt kicked the body remains around like a floppy rag doll just for his amusement, laughing as parts of her flew off or as limbs snapped until there was nothing left but her head. Warren described the behaviour as sickening and appalling as Grunt made them watch as a lesson for what could happen to others were careless and if they made similar errors. One foot Warren is definitely backing our cause to overthrow these despicable bullies now as are most of his co-workers.

I was so furious, I nearly went after Grunt myself but I was held back by Shuffling Kate who assured me to wait, my time would come. Acting in anger would not help our cause at this stage. One Foot Warren then told me that he'd personally had to take her still cognisant head to the dumping pit, although, as he knew it was my wife, he'd tried to put her in a dignified place to the side and upright so she wouldn't have to spend an eternity staring at other lumps of moaning flesh whilst upside-down. That's a fate worse than death in my book. It would have been more a mercy just to crush her head and be done with it. It sounds amazing her head even survived.

I tried desperately to scream in frustration, but Mungo caught me doing it. Ironically, he applauded me for producing what he thought was a fantastically scary moan with intimidating face. In fact, he has organised for me to do a workshop on this next week for all the new starters. I was going to try and get out of it, but then I thought that would be the perfect opportunity to influence the recently undead and inform them of what was really going on. They might be powerful, but I'm finding these Supers are not actually that bright. The military background might explain that, used to taking orders, not thinking and giving them.

I could feel the beginnings of the resistance movement starting to gain momentum because if colleagues like One foot Warren were being made to suffer as much as the rest of us, then feelings against these megalomaniacal super-mutant zombies would only be getting stronger and stronger.

Fear can only rule for so long until someone stands up to them and says 'no'.

That someone would be me.

Maybe this freak event of me regaining my memories and feelings wasn't a mistake after all. Maybe it has given me the purpose I was destined to fulfil all along. I have a bigger purpose. And the fate of my wife is just the catalyst.

I needed to stop this war and save human-kind from extinction, if only to save us from ourselves.

<u>Whispering</u>

Back home in the basement, I'd started to feel a little bit better. This was the only refuge we had from the Supers. They like to congregate together at the top of tower blocks in nearby cities and towns, up in the sky so they think they can look down on us. With them, though, it is more a case of 'out of sight, out of mind'. So it was good down here.

It appeared their telepathy had some limits after all, as they needed to focus on a particular individual to filter their thoughts from the general background noise of the masses. At least down here, among the horde, you could relax without one of them poking around inside your head.

As I looked around, it seemed our numbers were starting to thin a little bit. What with one offensive after another, my basement buddies had probably succumbed to bullets, blades and bombs or the wrath of the Supers' tempers themselves and we weren't being replaced.

As it was still light outside, there was a shaft of sun coming in from a high level window and hitting one of the newcomers we've called Bullet-magnet Ben from behind. He was creating and interesting poker colander pattern on the floor in front of him that changed as he swayed. I think he did that on purpose just to show off.

I'd been quietly testing the water by whispering my concerns over the way things have transpired recently under the heel of our oppressors with my fellow damp dwellers and I got the distinct feeling that they were thinking the same things as me. They didn't want to be responsible for human genocide either, they were beginning to understand the paradox now, and that the ongoing oppression of the Supers is giving zombie-kind an even worse reputation than the one it had already got (as if it could get any worse).

Of course, I'd only been saying this to the fellows I could trust, which was mainly my immediate basement circle (who I may say are doing very well at surviving so far thanks to our avoidance tactics), the veterans (any survivor from before the time of the Supers), and the recently deceased, as they had either seen too much or too little. There were a few among us, like Skull-chomp Ken over there, who were the radical, hardcore types and they actually aspired to see the Supers' plans through, even desired to be like them. They thought if they worked hard enough the Supers would let them become part of their collective and would give them access to the radiation source. Poor misguided fools. Perhaps Ken might find he'd had a slight accident soon, zombie's heads fall on broken pipes all the time. His disappearance wouldn't be noticed. Since they had got rid of all the counsellors for the recently deceased, I'd taken it upon myself to secretly try and fill the role for all the newcomers who had been recently turned under the new training role Mungo has given me. But rather than brainwash them with the virtues of zombie society, and I use that term loosely now, and put them through the trials I had to go through, I'd been educating them with a more balanced perspective and our need to advance beyond our culture. I tried to show them we needed to grow. Also, as many of them retained a lot of human memory and emotion immediately after changing, I'd been trying to help them keep hold of that, hold on to their humanity and develop a sympathy towards 'human rights' before we made them go extinct.

This had been very difficult as they have had to fight the overwhelming urges for brains that I remember oh so well. Some of them couldn't take it all in and went mad, which had often happened in the past. To be fair, we put those ones out of their misery with a quick spike through the head before the Supers got their hands on them and made them suffer more. We'd even managed to have a meeting in the corner of the basement the other night and share some views and feelings.

I'm pretty sure that had never been done before, but I got the feeling it was the start of something, a movement that we could take part in and control. If the Supers found out about this, we'd be in serious trouble.

I was shuffling over to the corner now for another meeting. There was quite a gathering already, I'm sure this would turn out to be quite interesting.

I'm sure that in my past, as a human, I'd been a public speaker at medical conferences, but I never thought that I'd be giving a speech to incite a revolution. If I was able, I would probably be nervous.

They were all looking at me very expectantly.

Well, I had started this; I had better be prepared to follow it through.

Here goes.

Fellow zombies…

Campaign for Peace

I'd come up with a campaign for Human Rights.
It still seemed a funny term to me now, as its meaning has
changed dramatically since it was first introduced by those
liberal Europeans so long ago. No longer was their right to have
a fair way of life, we were now talking about their right to
survive.
Slowly, but surely, I'd been building up support amongst my
companions and colleagues as we had been spreading the word
gently and secretly among the newly turned recruits and the
grisly old veterans; primarily as they carried the most sympathy
for the humans plight.
Our numbers of supporters were growing and I seemed to have
become the unofficial leader of the movement. This was not
something I'd really wanted, I was never a natural leader, but it
was something I had to come to terms with and be prepared to
do. It also seemed that I am the only one with a memory of my
pre-zombie state and have the cognitive ability to actually think
and plan anything in any complex detail. This would come as a
bit of a surprise to the Supers as they think they are 'all
knowing', but as discovered recently, they're not as clever as
they think they are. The intelligence of my colleagues varies
depending on how long they've been turned and how they were
thoroughly they were instructed upon turning, but all of them
are still guided by some base emotion of right or wrong and it
was my purpose to help them see which is which.
Our recently self-imposed leaders would have us either
decapitated or incinerated if they ever found out what we were
planning, or even discussing for that matter, for what they
would consider treasonous beliefs against our almighty leader,
Muto. But we were not to be deterred.
Genocide is inhumane, another shrewd and twisted term in this
day and age, and we were willing to sacrifice what was left of

our miserable, decrepit selves to protect these defenceless human beings with slowly decreasing numbers.

Our secret campaign had been growing gaining extra momentum over the last few months as stories were shared between the lower orders, you know, us normal zombies. Tales of bullying, violence and cruelty from above, the removal of our democratic rights, the loss of our support facilities, unfair death quotas, the lack of replacements as our own numbers dwindled and worst of all the amount of slaughter we were forced to carry out in the name of their cause. Not to mention the atrocities we've had to witness at the hands of the Supers too; their noble mission - to wipe out all resistance against their total domination of the world.

Within a very short time there would be no humans left at all. Already, it was becoming harder and harder to find any. They had either gone underground, to the mountains or were out at sea, all places we couldn't reach. This meant that eventually there would be none of us left either. Why couldn't the Supers see that? Were they so blind in their hatred of the last suffering survivors of the apocalypse?

Merely campaigning for reason and initiating democratic talks would never work with this dictatorship, they didn't understand 'talking'; it was action that was required. I know the old system before the coup wasn't perfect, but at least it had worked; it had a purpose and a cause and was orderly and efficient.

We were now going to stage a coup of our own taking out these evil leaders and their murderous regime to bring about some sense of peace and all of this was to help our so called mortal enemy.

Every human had a right to survive even if our kind was trying to obliterate them from the face of the earth. They had suffered for long enough and should be given a chance to at least recover for, as I have said before, their extinction meant our extinction. I held a belief, albeit a fragile one, that maybe both races could co-exist somehow. If we could ever cure the hunger for human brains, that is, that would make an interesting education programme and was probably our main obstacle to overcome. So, I'd gathered together my most trusted, well, I suppose you could call then 'generals' in these circumstances for want of a better word. These were a mixture of recently turned individuals that had held on to some of their human emotions and a group of veterans that, although they'd done their fair share of killing, had seen the light and a better way forward. In the dim light of the underground basement we used as our headquarters, I looked around at the assembled group. There was Trembling Pete, One-handed Harry, Stiff-back Joe, Shuffling Kate, Footdrag Norman, Wobbling Bob, V-legs Jane and our newest member Educated Emma, the teacher that I'd saved at the school. You'd never seen such a rotten, mouldy, bug-ridden bunch in your life but they all had one thing in common – they wanted to save the humans from extinction. Educated Emma had been extremely helpful as she'd managed to retain a lot of her memory, with my help, and it turned out her teaching speciality was history. We now had been taught about historical precedents of revolutions that we could draw from as well as some forgotten military tactics. These ideas may have been old, but the Supers certainly wouldn't know about them which essentially made them new again.

In the history of zombie society (much of which we will never know), this was as radical as it was going to get.

The starter plan was simple.

Firstly, we had to take out the radical extremists loyal to the Supers' cause as they would soon inform on us if they caught wind of what we are doing.

Secondly, we needed to take down one of the Supers and make it look like an accident as not to raise the suspicion of the others. We needed to know their strengths and weaknesses and just had to know if it could be done. I knew the perfect target for that one.

Thirdly, should the other two points go to plan, we needed to seed the generals into other units to form splinter groups and provide training and information that could then take down other Supers.

Should all these ideas be successful, we had to go after the leader himself, Muto. That would take numbers as surely by the time he'd seen most of his lieutenants disappear, even he would work out something was going on and become extremely dangerous.

All that alone was hard enough but, should we succeed in taking out the dictator and his cronies, the hardest task of all then had to be accomplished.

We would have to make peace with the humans.

Run Away

For God's sake, why wouldn't they shut up?

That incessant, repetitive moaning just went on and on and on. It was the worst torture that could have ever been imagined. It penetrated your skull and drilled into your brain, even when you covered your ears there was no escape from the continuous, dull, monotonous, deep hum of groaning. I was pretty sure it was sending me insane.

Occasionally it sounded like they were actually trying to make words that almost sounded like 'brains' or 'kill all humans', but maybe I was just hearing things, my mind playing tricks on me in revenge for the punishment it was enduring. It had been a long time since I'd slept; I was probably just imagining it. The barricade of furniture in the stairwell was still holding them back for now, but I could hear them working at it, methodically dragging bits and pieces away. At one point, there was a sudden shift in the pile followed by a slump and it sounded as if one or two of them may have been crushed under it judging by the bone snapping and fleshy squelching sounds that filtered through. A noise that came through all too clearly. My wife and son jumped and started whimpering again.

However, even that didn't stop them. Even a thing like losing one of their numbers wasn't going to stand in the way of them getting to us. They were inhuman, unstoppable machines.

I looked around for what felt like the twentieth time to analyse our position. My wife and son had situated themselves in the master bedroom and wrapped themselves in a blanket, hugging each other tightly for comfort. The exhaustion manifested as red eyes, grey skin and deep eye sockets. We were probably starting to look like our attackers.

I was standing vigil at the top of the stairs waiting to defend them should any one of those undead creatures finally manage to break through. I was assuming the house was full of them by now, all clambering over one another to get to their first victim.

I still had my sword that I'd carried with me upstairs, still smeared with the black, syrupy blood of the one I'd dismembered in the living room. Only now I realised it had a terrible reek, sweet like rotted meat, and I started to gip. I tip-toed swiftly into the bathroom and ran the blade under the tap whilst holding my breath, before wiping it clean on the curtain as the towels had gone down the stairs with everything else.

CRUNCH.

SQUELCH.

Another furniture cascade. Another splat. Another undead casualty.

At the rate they were working, I realised they'd be through very soon, probably within an hour or so. We'd thrown everything we could at them and there was no more furniture left unless we started dismantling the bathroom. Although they were relentless, it seemed they lacked the capability to be organised so they weren't doing a very good job.

By now I was so fatigued, I wasn't even sure I had the energy to fight them should they break through anyway. One or two of them maybe, but any more? No chance.

My thoughts turned towards attempting some sort of escape. It now appeared to be our only option of survival; we couldn't wait them out here.

There'd been hundreds of them emerging from the surrounding forest, so I didn't have any idea of how many there were outside. I went from window to window in every upstairs room, peering out into the gloom, to check on their numbers. As suspected by the number of shadows in the moonlight, they surrounded most of the house.

We did have the fire escape route that we always had in case of emergencies. This involved exiting the back bedroom window onto the porch roof just below it. That was just above the back door. Then it would involve jumping for safety from there into the garden. The porch roof was quite low so it was a fairly easy jump to make without fear of injury. This would seem our best way to exit except for the violent, murdering horde gathered in the garden below. What I needed was some way of dispersing them out enough to clear a path allowing us to charge through them, and then maybe we could just disappear into the woods and get up to the mountains as previously planned. I desperately started searching through the built-in cupboards and bedrooms looking for any inspiration on how I could achieve this. However, clothes, shoes and bedding were hardly going to put the fear of God into these things, never mind scatter them. I needed something drastic…

BANG.

CRACK.

…and fast.

My eyes wandered in vain when they eventually fell upon the loft hatch above me. Why hadn't I thought of that before? We could possibly hide up there. But what was the point? We wouldn't last up there for long without food or water anyway; they'd just wait us out. Perhaps there would be something stored up there that I could use?

I reached up and undid the catch, releasing the door and revealing the foldaway ladder. Dragging this down, I fixed it in place on the landing and then ascended into the drafty, dark above. With the power still off, I had no way to see where I was going, so I stretched out my arms and stumbled around, working from a mental plan, just hoping to land my hands on anything useful at all.

I cursed several times as fingers, elbows and knees bumped into various sharp corners. Old records, toys, pictures, chests of memorabilia, all things of great personal value, yet counted for nothing in the current crisis. Nostalgia would have no part to play in the coming future. Then, when I'd almost given up…

'Ouch, you bast…hang on…oh, yes.'

Fireworks, I'd forgotten about these.

They were left over from the New Year's party we had here at the end of last year with the family. These undead creatures were susceptible to fire, that's why the government and the army had been incinerating them. Some form of explosion might just be powerful enough to scatter them as well or at least create a worthy diversion. Maybe I could create a little firestorm of my own and take a few of them out. Hopefully, at least enough to clear us a path on our exit route and make a break for it.

I dragged the large cardboard box down the steps. When I got to the bottom, my wife and son were there waiting for me curious to see what I was up to. Suddenly, the box slipped from my fingers and landed with a bump on the floor. There was vigorously renewed moaning and scratching and the furniture barrier slumped again.

'What have you got there, love?' my wife asked wearily. Her red bloodshot eyes looked at me questioningly. I opened the box to reveal the contents, dozens of various fireworks and a tin box.

'Fireworks. We're going to blast our way out.' I tried to ignite some enthusiasm.

'Yes!' exclaimed my son seeing the possibility. But then he asked the devastating question, 'But Dad, how are we going to light them?'

My heart sank. How was I going to light them? The matches were in the kitchen and the path to the kitchen lay through dozens of undead creatures and a blockaded stair.

'Oh, shit! What a stupid idea.' I slumped to the floor in defeat.

'Look in the bathroom cabinet, sweetheart,' said my wife. 'I keep some matches in there for the candles.'

'Yes, you beauty!' I jumped up, planted a big kiss on her lips, and then went straight to the mirrored cabinet on the bathroom wall. Sure enough, there was a small matchbox. When I checked the contents there were only four left. Better make these count, I thought.

'Son, we are going to make a bomb. But don't tell your friends at school, ok?' I doubted it would be a long time before any schools started again, but as a parent it was just one of those things you said automatically whenever doing anything naughty.

'He looked at me excitedly knowing this was probably the only time I would ever say that and let him be part of it. At least it took his mind off the fear for a while. We needed action.

The idea was simple. Empty all the gunpowder into the tin box, seal it, and then create a fuse using one from a firework. We would then light this, throw it into the garden and the resulting explosion would either knock over or ignite the undead humans long enough to create a window of opportunity for us to jump off the porch roof, cross the garden and enter the forest beyond or it would be an almighty flop and we would be trapped here to await our fate. It was risky at best, suicidal at worst, but I was willing to try anything right now, just to get us out of here. I was desperate; desperate to save my family in any way possible.

Me and my son set to work dismantling fireworks and soon had the tin box half full with gunpowder. Concentrating on the task had worked in distracting my son for the time being and even my wife's defeated posture changed slightly to one more of hope. I used the taper from a catherine wheel to act as a fuse poking this through the lid of the box and we sealed it tight. It was a complete botch job, but then, aren't they the most dangerous kind?

'Right. Wrap up. Bring those blankets. Put on some extra clothes, we could be out for some time. Get ready, this is it.' Both my wife and son looked understandably apprehensive. Now the reality of what we were doing struck home my stomach was doing somersaults and I could taste acid rising up my throat.

Just as we prepared to leave, I checked my pocket again to make sure the Zeta 16 was still there. Then this made me think of something else. With the only possible cure with me, and no certainty of my outcome, I thought it best to leave some indication of were we were going and what I had with me should someone come seeking survivors up here.

Quickly nipping into the office room I pulled a pen, piece of paper and a brown manila envelope out from one of the built-in cupboards and began swiftly scribbling. When I was done, I simply pinned it to the wall. I wanted to make it obvious to anyone entering that it had been placed there intentionally and not fallen on the floor by accident. I sincerely doubted anyone would ever find it, but I felt better inside for doing it. People had a right to know what happened to their only possible redemption and my selfishness of taking it with me. It helped clear my conscience slightly.

That task completed, we gathered ourselves, mentally and physically, our supplies, our makeshift bomb and the few remaining matches and climbed tentatively out through the back bedroom window onto the porch roof trying to be as quiet as possible.

Despite our caution, it was almost as if they knew we were coming as the moaning seemed to increase in pitch and volume. It was like they were erupting into frenzy.

'Ready?' I said to the two shadows beside me.

'Yes,' came two short, nervous squeaks.

I pulled a match and struck it.

It lit. There was a slight breeze.

The match went out.

'Shit!'

I tried a second match but I as I was striking it, my hands were shaking so much, I lost my grip and it slipped from my hand into the gutter.

'Oh crap!'

Two matches left. Never had I felt so much pressure over such a small simple task.

This time I was careful. With slow motion exaggeration, I struck it. It lit.

I shakily moved it towards the fuse and it caught, fizzing dramatically into life. Worryingly, the fuse started going down quicker than I'd thought it would and I panicked by grabbing the tin and throwing it hastily into the garden below.

BOOM!

My ears rang. The garden was lit for a brief moment.

We had all diverted our eyes from the massive flash but I managed to briefly see the hundreds of reflecting eyes staring back. I involuntarily passed wind. The explosion rocked the porch roof knocking us backwards and a several tiles slipped taking the guttering with them.

We fought to catch our breath.

Then, after a few moments, I peered over the edge.

There was a muddy crater in what was left of quite a large garden, rimmed with flame and debris, and the blast had knocked back and decapitated some of the horde below as hoped. Many humanoid shaped torches were also staggering about, lighting their comrades; all the better to light our way. And there it was – our escape route; a large clearance of the horde that we could get through.

'This is it, come on, now.'

Sliding tentatively to the edge, I lowered my legs and jumped first, landing with a roll. I sprung up immediately, sword still in hand held ready, prepared to fend off any attacker.

My wife followed, and then my son and I caught him to prevent him falling towards the creatures. Their dismembered arms outstretched, ready to pounce.

There was no hanging around. I grabbed hold of my family's hands and dragged them as quickly as possible into the darkened maw of the gaping black forest. We vanished into the black.

The End of Mungo

We'd been scouting for weeks.

This was a deep recon mission, far, far away from our central base of operations. Far away from the nice damp basement of home which, to be honest, I could really use right now. You see, Mungo has brought us deep into the country's interior, towards all the high mountains and rolling hills, where the Supers think there'll be hundreds of humans hiding away stupidly thinking we won't know where they are.

We're not stupid, you know. You'd think that just by reaching higher ground you could survive. But we know how rugged and exposed it is up there and especially how barren and cold it can be. You'd have to come down for food and water eventually, and guess what? Yep, we'd be right there, waiting for you and we can wait a very, long, long time. At a push, some of us can climb as well, so beware.

We'd actually been brought on this mission, my cohorts and me, as punishment, would you believe? Mungo had lost his second in command position competition to Grunt (that evil bastard) and, to be honest, he was pretty pissed off. In fact, he didn't even make runner up but actually came last out of all the Supers in terms of human conversions and kills for those under his command. In other words, us lot!

After mauling, smashing, vaporising and throwing around half my colleagues, who were just unlucky enough to be in his vicinity when he found out, in a fit of pure anger and rage that had us basically fearing for our unlives. Fortunately, when he realised how decimated his ranks were becoming; he eventually calmed down and stopped. It didn't do us any good though.

As punishment for doing so badly, Muto ordered him to send his troops on the furthest expeditions (one of those where my kind rarely came back) and to command them personally. Yes, personally. He was coming with us. Oh, he didn't like that, I can tell you.

However, it did for us present an opportunity, one that we'd been hoping would happen for quite some time – the chance to get Mungo out on his own and away from the other Supers and away from their source of power.

This could be our chance to take him down.

So, we'd been swaggering across the countryside for days now, the hills, streams and dry stone wall becoming a monotonous blur. These days were long and the sun was high in the sky, so I guess you could call it Summer. Lovely weather, you might say. Yeah, nice for you humans maybe, but to us, it was terrible. I was severely starting to dry out. So much so, sometimes I would crackle when I walked and every time there was any sort of breeze, dust clouds come streaming off me. I was flaking like a week old sausage roll. Occasionally, we'd found some streams or rivers to dip into, just to dampen and re-hydrate ourselves. The limbs started to loosen up a bit after that. But when it was really sunny, without a cloud in the sky and the suns rays were belting down, we had to shelter in the shade of the trees and buildings.

Amazingly, despite the distance we'd covered, we hadn't come across any signs of life at all, human or animal. Where had all the farm animals gone? In a rural place like this you'd expect to see at least a few cows or sheep.

This truly was an apocalypse.

We saw many abandoned cars covered in several months' worth of dirt and dust. One vehicle looked like it had been there so long, even weeds were growing on it. Nature was starting to reassert itself without the humans to hold it at bay with long grasses and weeds, trees spreading and verges starting to spread into the roads.

Houses and shops in small villages all had open doors and smashed windows. There was evidence of looters everywhere. Other properties had been burned down and here and there were the occasional corpse of human and zombie alike, rotting away and full of maggots and flies, stuck in the poses of some violent death or final agonising conflict. No doubt disease would have spread should anyone have remained.

The hills and mountains were fairly close now and were beginning to rise around us on all sides. We tended to follow the valleys as these contained the roads, rivers and the easiest level route for us to navigate. We also proceeded on the assumption that humans would also work their way down to water sources at some point and we could surprise and capture them by the rivers and streams. These particular ones here would probably be fresh as they were supplied by the nearby springs in the mountains unlike the supplies in the cities.

I say we were going to capture them, but that wasn't really going to happen.

There was a reason why Mungo had picked our particular band. The usual faces were here: Trembling Pete, One-handed Harry, Stiff-back Joe, Shuffling Kate, Footdrag Norman, V-legs Jane and Educated Emma. Mungo couldn't prove it, but we knew he suspected us of being the ones that let him down with the kill numbers and if we ever let down our mental guards long enough for him to read our minds closely, he'd find out he was right.

That had been our first minor victory against him. We'd been secretly saving humans and not killing them, or hiding and falling for weeks in the hope it would not only save a few souls but scupper his promotion as well, and it had worked. So what if it got us sent on this mission? It was a small price to pay. At least it got us, and more importantly him, away from the killing zones. It would at least ease our consciences a little more.

At first he had marched us rather sharply, him pushing us from the rear with his normal fury and anger, firing fire-bolts at our heels to get us moving. The original pace had been relatively, for us, blistering. But now, we'd noticed, as time progressed, he began to fall more and more behind, the bolts became less

frequent and he became quieter and quieter. His feet weren't
lifting that high either.

We, us normal ones, could carry on regardless, it was what we
did, but he didn't seem to have our kind of stamina. That was
when it occurred to me – he'd not got his radioactive source to
power him up anymore. As he got further away from it, he
started reverting back to one of us, but an increasingly
weakened version. During his time as a Super he must have put
increased wear and tear on his body and now it was just starting
to manifest due to the lack of regeneration. At this moment, he
could probably still rip one of us apart with his bare hands or
blast us to smithereens, but it was my guess that he was
reserving his power for either any humans we came across or
the long journey back.

If he made it back.

I'd stored that useful titbit of information with the aim of
sharing it with my colleagues later on. If we wanted to stop the
Supers for good, we'd eventually have to go after that same
source of power, the irradiated area of the bomb site, and that
wouldn't be easy considering the Supers jealously guarded it. It
was interesting to know they weakened when away from it.
Anyway, that was for the future, we had to get through this
predicament first.

Passing through yet another nondescript, small rural village
(they were all beginning to look the same), which was as
devastated as the rest, there was a crossroads with a few roads
all leading towards various hillscapes surrounding it situated in
the centre. Nature had already begun to reclaim the place with
overgrown verges, weeds appearing through cracks in the road
and tree branches reaching in through broken windows.

V-legs Jane had spotted some recent tyre marks heading off in
one direction and was doing her best to distract Mungo and
divert him away from them by wandering in the opposite
direction and making a big fuss, but unfortunately it didn't
work. He'd spotted them. Fresh tyre marks meant survivors;

survivors who'd probably been here to stock up on supplies,
tools or water from the stream and taken them back to their
hideout.

Seeing the tracks and considering all the walking we'd done I
thought to myself, wouldn't it be nice if I could still drive and
then I thought, maybe I could. I'd recently handled a rocket
launcher with some aplomb; surely I could recall how to drive.
Granted, my reactions weren't what they once were, but there
would be no pedestrians or traffic on the road to worry about
anyway. Yes, there was the occasional traffic crash, road block
or abandonment blocking the way, but I was sure there'd be a
way around those. Even a couple of miles in a car would reduce
our travelling time by a day or two. I'd have to think about that,
again, if we got out of this predicament.

So refreshed by the new chase, Mungo mentally urged us along
the recently used road and toward the stern and severe looking
set of limestone crags and rises that stood against the bright
blue sky almost saying to us, 'come on then, we've stood here
for eons, how are you going to defeat us?' It was my hope that
it wouldn't come to that.

The terrain started to ascend more rapidly underfoot as we left
the main village and we began to see more evidence of human
activity. A footprint here, disturbed stones there, it would seem
they had got a bit complacent having not been visited by their
friendly neighbourhood zombies for a while. They'd not even
covered their tracks. It is known that we are excellent trackers.
How do you think we always find you when you're hiding? It's
not just luck.

We found the parked vehicle at the end of a country lane where
it was obvious by the footprints that the passengers had got out,
gone through a gate and proceeded up the hill. The tracks
clearly led up the trails in the hillside, obvious paths that were
used on a regular basis. They were originally tourist paths,
perhaps, as they were well maintained with stone and gravel.
Our intrepid leader pointed and telepathically ordered us to go

forth up the rise, so in single file we started to make our way. If you think walking on the flat ground is slow, it was excruciatingly tedious going up on a rapidly ascending path. Yet we plodded along on our monotonous march, weaving around boulders and scree. We'd snaked our way up a couple of hundred metres when, looking back, I'd suddenly realised, Mungo wasn't with us. Unbelievably, he'd stayed at the foot of the hill and, as we looked down, he appeared to be…sitting… with his head between his knees. That was bizarre. Maybe this was the time to do something about him at last if the body language was anything to go by. If we didn't know better, we'd say he was exhausted.

Thinking carefully about it, still trying not to give ourselves away mentally even at this range, we carried on our mountain trek. As we rounded some crags and avoided some perilous looking drops to our left that headed towards pancake city, I'd become aware of something, no someone, watching us. Looking up, sure enough, there was a shaggy head with a young pair of deep-set eyes peeping over the edge of a ledge.

Those eyes suddenly looked startled upon being discovered and, in a flash a young boy appeared and decided it was time to flee. Obviously a look-out, he must have started back to warn his friends or family. However, in his haste, his foot slipped and he lost his grip and before we knew it, he'd landed in a heap before us, seriously banging his head on a rocky outcrop with a sickening crunch, knocking him unconscious.

A painful flashback suddenly hit me. My son. A similar fate. I was unable to save him.

Where did that come from? Something similar to what I'd just seen? Yes, but involving my son. How had that happened? I didn't have time to contemplate it, it would have to wait until later, but it was a weird sensation and I would have to find out what it meant.

Well, you might take a guess at what we did next, a harmless, innocent victim at our mercy, but you'd be wrong. None of us wanted to harm this boy, especially me. In fact, I wanted to get him aid, save him and help him survive. This was all part of our new ethos. We were undoubtedly on the right track towards the human encampment otherwise why would they need scouts, so I knew we had to get him there for urgent medical attention. Gently, and as nimbly as I could for a decaying bag of bones, I scooped him up, cradling him in my flimsy arms as best I could, and led the rest of the band onwards and upwards hoping the humans would be somewhere nearby.

It took some time but we eventually stumbled upon the human camp. They had found a sheltered basin within the hills surrounded by some tall rock formations that provided shelter and set up camp with some fairly modern looking camping gear. They had a good view all around and it was quite defensible with only two ways in our out through the rocks yet no-one had even detected our arrival. They must have been heavily reliant on the lookouts to not have watches so close to camp. There were around twenty to thirty people of varying ages all milling around a central campfire and, as it was turning evening by now, they were attempting to light it and prepare a meal looking at the equipment they were using.

One of them spotted us.

Instantly there was uproar.

They were pretty surprised to see us, as you'd imagine. A small band of undead lurching into their sanctuary quite openly, and they'd not even been warned by their scout. One woman screamed and pointed directly at me when she realised I was carrying their lookout in my arms, I guessed it may have been her son by the similarities in their looks. There were pangs of anguish on her face.

The men ran to gather weapons, guns, knives and makeshift spears; they didn't even look comfortable holding weapons, but stood back as they were unsure as to why we were carrying the boy in such a fashion. By now we'd normally be tucking in. We stopped.

Trembling Pete held his hand up in front of him and towards them showing his palm – the sign to wait – then together the two of us edged slowly forward. You could see the shock and suspicion all over their faces, white of eyes and gritted teeth. There were tense, nervous and agitated postures. I gently lowered the boy to the ground, putting him onto his side in the recovery position (something else I'd remembered from medical training) and pointed to his head wound. Then Trembling Pete waved his hand towards himself summoning the humans forward.

They undoubtedly understood but their response was a mixture of fear, confusion and mistrust. Who could blame them? We hardly had the best reputation of trustworthiness. When was the last time you were greeted by zombies with hugs and kisses? Cautiously, one of the men edged forward, kneeled down and examined the boy; his eyes were always darting back to us. We stood gently swaying, our arms by our sides, making no threatening movements.

After a quick once-over, the man could obviously see the boy's injuries but more importantly seemed content there were no bite marks on him. He looked at us again and I nodded, hopefully showing reassurance. The man seemed to understand that and scooped up the boy, carrying him back to the rest of his group. A few of the others accompanied him fetching medical supplies and boiling water.

I guess this was the first gesture of compassion and goodwill we, zombie kind, had ever shown. A tiny gesture, I agree, but it made me feel good. It made all of us feel good.

Deciding we'd been up here long enough, and seeing that the boy was receiving medical care, we thought it was time we should make our way back down. No point in prolonging their agony. We would just report we'd found nothing to Mungo and be on our way towards some other village. I mean, how would he know? He never came up and the way he'd looked suggested he wouldn't be coming anyway.

But then, unbelievably, at the top of the path, there he was.
Mungo had come and he looked mad!

This would definitely shatter the small amount of trust we'd just achieved with the campers. Especially when Mungo went nuts and decided he was going to kill them all.

The humans, spotting this new threat, immediately took up arms again and began screaming instructions sensing this immediate threat. Hostility pierced the air. It was my guess that they'd seen one of the Supers before.

Mungo stormed forward and stood in front of me just taking a moment to survey his latest victims to be. His hands started glowing as he readied his fire bolts.

No! I wasn't going to let that happen.

I acted first.

I raised my hands and, with a massive roundhouse swing, struck him on the back of the head.

The humans were stunned.

My colleagues were stunned.

But most importantly, Mungo was stunned – and fell over flat on his face.

I jumped, or more like toppled, on top of him, grabbed hold of his head by the ears and started rotating and twisting his neck. Mungo's arms were flailing and random fire bolts were flying through the air striking rocks and earth and getting too close to the humans for my liking. My colleagues, seeing my bravery, risked themselves too and grabbed his arms, Foot-drag Norman taking a full bolt in the stomach and falling apart before the rest of them got a good grip and ripped his arms off completely. That stopped the bolts.

As suspected, he was definitely weaker, and with great effort I pulled off his head with a crack and a sucking pop. It slipped through my fingers and rolled towards the humans. The body went limp under me but of course the head wasn't dead. Mungo was telepathically yelling every curse under the sun at us and what the outcome of this insubordination would be if the other

Supers ever found out. However, I knew this wouldn't get back to the other Supers because at the distance we'd covered, they'd never hear him.

As the head gnashed and growled in front of the armed men, they looked upon it with a mixture of horror and revulsion. One of them leaned over to vomit. But another stepped forward with a long hunting knife and sunk it up to the hilt through one of the eye sockets. That did the trick. I gave him big thumbs up.

And thus was the end of the mighty Mungo.

It was a great feeling. It had been simpler than I thought, but then Mungo was obviously weakened. But maybe, just maybe, we had a chance to put an end to this stupid war after all. They weren't as invincible as we thought, we'd proved that now.

I looked one more time at the human camp; envied them, felt sorry for them and then felt relieved that at least some of their kind had survived. My colleagues and I all turned to descend the hill and, after a short descent, as I looked back, there lined up on the edge, they watched us go. I couldn't be sure, but I think one of them waved goodbye.

Shortly afterwards, the body of Mungo tumbled down the hill via the cliff face to be smashed on the jagged rocks and crags below.

The walk back down seemed a little bit easier after that.

<u>We're Coming</u>

We were feeling pretty good about ourselves right now,
mentally, of course, not physically. Well, at least I was,
sometimes it's difficult to tell with the others. Our aims and
objectives may be the same, but it's hard to show any emotion
visibly when your face is contorted in the shape of some sort of
horror mask. I could only go off what they were telling me.
We'd descended the mountain in one piece, unlike Mungo,
whose parts were now scattered at its base after what can only
be called a route one descent. The humans had made sure of
that, which was probably just as well, as it's not a good idea to
have a radioactive, decaying corpse hanging around your
hidden mountain campsite. Not good for the old human health.
So what now?
Bring down more of the Supers? We felt like we could do that
now. Make peace with more humans? We'd have to find them
first. Was that a temporary peace we made there? I really hoped
so, although the latest event was just one tiny drop in the ocean
compared to the overall task. I guess we'd just have to take it
one lurching step at a time. Thinking over the incident though,
it was lucky that they came across us and not any of our
unsympathetic counterparts, the whole affair could have ended
a lot differently.
Ok, so we'd brought down one Super. Well done us! But he
was far away from his radioactive power source and, as a result,
greatly weakened. We'd also had the element of surprise; the
big lug never saw it coming so arrogant he was in his
superiority. So we advised ourselves not to get too cocky. No
doubt it would be a different task entirely at radioactive super
mutant central.
Maybe that should be our next mission, to infiltrate their
radioactive power source and either destroy it so they could no
longer use it. Or capture it and use it for ourselves, mutate our

rebellion, to be rid of them on an equal footing. The latter was a dangerous path to go down as it was quite obvious to me that power corrupts or we wouldn't be in this situation in the first place, would we? I guess we'd have to cross that bridge when we came to it; we still had to find that source first. For now, we had a long way to go to make our way back to where we'd come from as that would need to be our starting point for any future venture. The place we now called home. Sometimes the lulling invite of that cold, dark, wet basement felt so appealing. It took us weeks to amble here and would take just as long to return.

At that moment, my earlier idea came back to me. Why don't we use a vehicle? Enough of my human memories had returned and I believed I should at least attempt it. On the other hand, although my mind was willing, I would still have to see if the body would cope. I reckoned that I would at least be able to get it into gear and manage if the road was fairly straight without too many bends or obstructions. Obviously, my reactions wouldn't be up to scratch for big bends or great speed, but I was certainly willing to give it a go.

My only other worry was trying to remember the way back. I'd seen some signage on the way but a lot of it had been destroyed or vandalised. We'd also not followed many roads as we were keeping our low profile via streams and tree lined routes. I suppose the main thing to do was follow the same principle back as we took to get here of following the valleys and rivers, or at least all the roads near them. I'd tried to spot some landmarks on our way, various hills and buildings and so on, just in case we did get the option to return, so I would have to try and navigate by them.

I looked around at my cohorts and wondered at the extent of their ability. Their hearts were mostly in the right place, (I don't think anyone had lost theirs yet though there may be a few puncture wounds), but they were prepared to follow me. Yet, still now, I seemed to be the only one who had any major memory recall from the before time and these guys could only register the odd flashback if they were lucky. I considered it was enough. Their ethics, their knowledge of right and wrong had been awakened and that was all I needed to know.

We retraced our steps back to the rural village where we'd first seen the human trail. If we were going to find a vehicle, it had to be big enough to transport several of us. This automatically ruled out a car. We needed a bus, or a truck, or something similar.

This was only a small isolated village and, as I scanned the scene, I wasn't hopeful of finding anything remotely suitable. There was nothing here…except…maybe that tractor and trailer. Yes!

Low speed, high elevation, all terrain - perfect. Surely we couldn't be so lucky. I led my colleagues over to check it out. Looking it over, it appeared quite modern, bright green and shiny with chunky black tyres and with hardly any mud on it. This farmer must have been doing well. Something urgent must have happened in the village because it had literally been abandoned and hadn't collected the dust and debris seen on other stranded vehicles. Maybe the campers had been using this vehicle as well recently, I couldn't be sure. The farmer may have even been one of the inhabitants of the mountain camp. And even better, the keys were still in the ignition, I couldn't believe our luck.

The big question that occurred to me now was, was there any diesel in it? We'd be stuffed without that. With a great degree of difficult creaking, stretching, pulling, pushing and a big shove up the backside from my friends, I was launched into the cab.

I plopped myself down into the chair. That felt a bit weird; I don't think I'd sat down for ages. My crunching, cracking, popping knees agreed. We rarely had the need for chairs, preferred to stay upright and sway. Educated Emma had to force my pelvis back just to get my bum in the seat, all ability to flex through the midriff long gone.

I instructed my clan to climb up onto the trailer which, in itself, was an event to behold. Luckily, it was a low-loader, so after plenty of ungainly scrambling, they were all aboard and stood with eyes forward looking at me in the cab and waiting for me to work my magic.

I thought, this had better work now.

With grimy fingers, I wrapped my digits around the keys and twisted. The engine rumbled into life. Awesome. I could feel expectant stares on the back of my head.

Then I worked the pedals and gear stick.

CRUNCH. GRIND. SQUEAK. CRACK. GRUNT…and that was just my joints, never mind the gears that I was trying to operate very badly. I dropped the handbrake, stepped lightly on the accelerator and…oomph!

A sudden halt.

I looked back to see my team, flat on their faces, toppled forward by the stalling. I guessed I needed a bit of a better touch on the clutch. Well, come on, it had been a while since I'd driven anything, never mind a tractor.

Turning the key again, the engine roared back to life. I turned round and noticed that my colleagues had all decided to stay down either sat or laying – wise decision. So they did learn quickly.

With creaking and groaning sinews I eased the pedals and with small, juddering movements we began to advance. After the stalling performance I was a bit hesitant to change gears but thought I should otherwise we'd run out of petrol in no time using the low gears. CRUNCH. BANG. GROAN (me and the gearbox again) and soon enough we were steadily on our way down the green country lanes bordered with stone walls, lush fields and picturesque hills. Checking the fuel gauge, I saw it was roughly half full. Ok, not bad. Even if we didn't get that far it would still be quicker than walking. I felt a small moment of triumph as we gently rumbled along and I navigated us around our first corner only just brushing the verge.

Now we just had to find our way home.

Super mutants – here we come!

<u>Ready Or Not…</u>

We'd found it.

We'd finally located the source of the Supers' power.

All the surrounding vegetation for miles around had withered and died leaving a stark grey silhouette on the horizon.

This area was really quiet with hardly any of our kind, the 'normals', around, that was our first clue. They'd obviously been sent on errands of conquering similar to the one we'd returned from in the countryside. I doubted many of them would return as we did. The others that were kept here are probably the Super's slaves, or whipping boys, should any of them feel the urge to give someone a beating.

The rest of our numbers must be scattered far and wide by now, the humans in this area would have diminished a long time ago. There was a strange buzz in the air that probably only our kind would be able to sense. It wasn't a tactile feeling as such, just more of a perception, as if some invisible force was piercing our bodies and our willpower was being increased to make our pitiful carcasses react and move with greater speed and agility. It was only a weak force at the moment though; we were still a way off the actual physical source of it.

The human side of me recognised this for what it was – radiation. I guessed that this would be from an unexploded bomb or missile launched against us in one last desperate attempt by the humans to rid them of our zombie plague. Even their weapons of mass destruction didn't stop us – only made us stronger.

Evidence showed that this place was jealously guarded by the Supers though. I deduced these would have been the initial zombies converted from the nuclear attack in this area. We still weren't sure of the actual numbers of these monsters, how many would be here or out on patrol leading units of other normal zombies like Mungo did with us. I knew they loved hunting humans but, as our expedition with Mungo showed, they probably didn't want to wander too far or they'd weaken. They were almost trapped which was another weakness we may be able to exploit should we need to. Go away – lose power, stay here – keep power but with no humans to smash.

I'd been wondering if news of the destruction or disappearance of Mungo had made its way back yet. Presumably not. He probably wouldn't even be missed as he was sent away as punishment anyway, never expected to return…just like us.

But we were back. Ha ha.

And we meant business.

Gazing from the distant, scorched and barren ridge we now occupied, I looked down upon the remains of a desolate city. We'd been here for a few days now, keeping it under surveillance, staying out of sight, trying to get some idea of what we were about to face.

I couldn't tell you the name of this town but it must have been of some importance considering the way it had sprawled and had executive, corporate looking high rises standing sentinel over the rest of the Victorian urban decay like the tyrant, in one of those towers, standing dictator and thinking himself superior over the rest of us all Muto - our primary target.

Our initial plan was fairly simple: sneak into the city, find the fallen nuclear weapon, charge ourselves up with radiation and find the Supers to fight them on their terms based loosely on what we'd planned back in the basement all those months ago. Sounded easy, right?

Wrong.

As we'd stood and watched over this ghost town, unnervingly we found that we could 'sense' the inhabiting super mutants; we could 'see' them. They had a glowing aura around them, visible from some considerable distance, and strangest of all, we could 'hear' their thoughts. This was only a mild sensation now but, as we were being affected by the radioactive fallout, I realised that these giveaway conditions would start happening to us too making it very difficult to sneak in anywhere. They'd easily see us coming. We also knew Muto, in his tower, would be able to see us from a mile away.

I could see him, every night, at the top of the tallest skyscraper, glowing like a beacon, a radioactive lighthouse in the dark. He'd know we were coming before we even reached the first step of that tower.

So, ok, let's face it, we didn't have a good plan.

It was on the fourth day of our vigil out on the ridge that inspiration finally came to me. Growing steadily stronger and more rejuvenated, we could feel the power building within us, even this far from the source. Trembling Pete had miraculously stopped trembling now and had even managed to launch a small firebolt from his hand. That was quite a shock for all of us, especially as he was only throwing a stone to test his arm. Shuffling Kate could now pick her feet up and V-legs Jane was now just, well, Jane. They all began to love their new-found mobility. It was like old age pensioners acting like teenagers.

It remained that I was still the only one who could plan any strategy as I was the only one with any memory of the time before and fully functioning mental ability, but the rest of them also appeared to be getting smarter as well in some small way so any plan of actions I devised would be acted out with some degree of competence.

Like a commander, I'd been looking for possible routes into the urban centre that would offer the least resistance and that was when I'd spotted something totally awesome that we could use. On one of the main roads on the fringe of the city limits, fairly near to our current position, were the remains of an army roadblock. I guessed this had been set up after our outbreak to try and contain our threat and protect the citizens upon their escape – little good that did them.

However, wherever there was anything military there would be weapons such as guns, blades, grenades and so on. Yes, I knew, they may have been pretty useless against our numbers in the hands of humans, but put them in the hands of a group of charged up super zombies and those Supers would never know what was coming. Where the humans were firing at us without control, we knew exactly where our own weak points were. We just had to believe that the Supers weren't totally indestructible this close to their power source.

Still, best of all, I saw one thing on that roadblock that would be our best weapon of all – a tank. Yes, a bloody tank. I'd remembered how to drive a tractor; I was more than prepared to have a go at driving one of those monstrous war machines with treads on. As I was becoming more mobile, so I was becoming more confident.

So, I visualised the scene - a group of pumped up 'normal' zombies, a rebellion, driving down the centre of town with weapons blazing, mowing down the Supers left and right and then placing one well-aimed rocket right up Muto's arse.

I scared myself at the hostility within me. I'd never even felt like this towards the humans even in my earliest days after being turned.

After a brief explanation, all my comrades were willing to commit themselves to this mission and die (again) trying if they had to.

Educated Emma, now my second in command, was, upon finding the bomb, elected to detonate it if it was still functional but only as a last resort. Even now, after all this time, she was still haunted by the school incident and was willing to sacrifice herself just to make up for the horror delivered to those children at the hands of Mungo as long as it took a few Supers with it. For someone as level headed as her – she wanted revenge.

As a group, we'd decided to wait one more day, get a little bit stronger without being detected, and begin our assault tomorrow just as it was getting light. The time of the day didn't really matter, but for some reason inside me, it just felt right. It was kind of poetic, attacking at dawn, a very human quality. Then there was this other strange sensation in my brain that wanted my body to react strangely, although it couldn't, until I rationally figured out what it was – nerves.

Anyway, wouldn't those Supers be surprised.

Dawn broke and we were ready. I was ready.

The sky had a grey light, and it was a dull, miserable and pouring down with rain. Well, maybe not that miserable, we were glad of the wet, it had re-hydrated us a little after the recent dry spell. We still needed the water to keep us moist even though we were regenerating, to stop us creaking and tearing and rustling so much. I kind of hoped that the rain might also mask our approach, make it harder for them to visually see us at least. I wasn't sure if rain could mask radiation. They would still, however, be able to detect us mentally on approach but, with so much practice against Mungo, we'd all become cerebrally disciplined and grown proficient in concealing our thoughts and blocking any metal intrusion.

It was now or never.

With our newly found strength and agility, we were now moving at a brisk walk although being careful not to slip on the muddy ground. After shuffling for so long, this almost felt like sprinting – we were flying. Moving along the ridge, I was leading the troop to the main road I'd seen the previous day. Once on the concrete we made an even swifter pace and soon came upon the military road block.

There were no dead, decaying bodies here, either these guys had turned into Supers, which would be dangerous as they would be trained soldiers, or they may have been vaporised by the Supers in some final conflict. I was inclined the think the former as there were no remnants or residues left indicating any extinguished life. I spotted one or two skeletons, obviously been picked clean by carrion eaters but they were of no consequence. Yet the most important thing we found were the various weapons and munitions scattered around the area, most likely where they had fallen, dropped by the dead soldiers or left by the Supers who thought themselves so superior that they didn't need weapons. There were rifles, grenades, hand guns, a couple of sub-machine guns, a mortar, boxes full of ammo and then, with glee, I found a rocket launcher.

Loading ourselves up, I flittered around the squad showing them how to work the various devices though I wouldn't let them fire anything. I didn't want to draw any unwanted attention towards us yet. In reality, there was little I could instruct apart from 'here's the trigger, aim, fire' or 'pull this ring, throw'.

Armed to the teeth (those of us that had them) it reminded me of an old film, which I comically renamed for our own purpose – Zombie Apocalypse Now. We were going to war.

I then turned my attention to the main piece of hardware that we'd come for, the tank. With some effort, I managed to climb on to the top only suffering a couple of skin scrapes. Luckily, the hatch had been left open, no doubt thanks to some escaping soldier fleeing the Supers or the hordes of zombies coming toward them ceaselessly. It was always the best option to run away in those circumstances.

I dropped down into it and orientated myself. There were still a few shells left, excellent, and no key was needed for the ignition, I just prayed that it had some fuel in it as well. Maybe this would be our lucky day after all, just one way to find out. Fumbling, I managed to press the ignition starter and the engine fired into life with a booming, rumble. There were levers instead of a steering wheel controlling the speed and direction of each caterpillar tread and there was a small hatch to see through. Surely this wouldn't be too hard. At least there weren't any pedestrians or other traffic on the road though; that could have got a bit messy.

Popping my head back up through the hatch, I gestured for my cohorts to climb aboard. With a lot of struggling and lurching under the weight of their weapons, they all managed to mount and sat themselves atop the metal hulk. One-handed Harry dropped in beside me and took the position in the gunners chair; the rest of them remained on top, for and aft, loading their weapons with ammo.

Time to bring the fight.

I dropped myself into the driver's seat, a little more agile than the last time I had driven, and went through the mentally prepared map in my head for the fastest way to Muto Towers. I looked at the shells and the rocket launcher by my side – these beauties had Muto's name written all over them. If I could, I would have smiled.

Pushing the levers forward, we rumbled into motion and after negotiating a few obstacles in the road, and when I say negotiated I actually mean drove over the top of them, I was soon getting used to driving the metal beast. I was keeping our progress slow and steady. I knew the Supers would know we were here by now, I could feel them, in my head, cautiously converging on our position all under orders from him upstairs. We all could. But my comrades were ready. I could sense their confidence and determination to fight the coming menace.

The thoughts coming from the Supers pleased me, you could sense their confusion. Who was driving the tank? All humans around here had been wiped out, hadn't they? Surely no-one is brave enough to attempt and assault on us, they've got no chance? Why can't we sense them properly?

But eventually the penny dropped and they could sense us, their underlings - 'normal' zombies – and they could sense our intent. How dare they stand up to our glorious leader? I think that worried them, we were setting a precedent for rebellion and that would not go down well with Muto. We almost felt his wrath burning down on us from his tower.

Initially, I started to pick our way through the war-torn devastated streets, weaving through cars and debris from buildings, but this was only slowing us down. So I decided on a more direct approach and rolled over or crashed through

whatever was in our way. Plus, this was more fun. Weird that –
I think I was enjoying myself.

The unexploded nuclear device, our first target, was situated in
the centre of the city, so I steered us through the bigger main
roads towards it. There had evidently been some big stand-offs
here, mainly at junctions, one last stand, funnelling the enemy
into the kill zone, as there was military hardware scattered all
over the place, plenty of dusty skeletons and small piles of
black ash, the remains of vaporised humans, no doubt.

Then the first Super appeared.

The next thing I knew about it was the eruption of gunfire from
above, just detectable above the noise of the engines. I stopped
the tank and heard something hit us from behind – after
checking there was no damage internally though.

Curious, I popped my head up through the hatch and looked to
the rear just in time to see a Super's head exploding into a
thousand pieces giving up under pressure from such an
onslaught of concentrated gunfire of my squad all going for the
weakest point. The headless body collapsed to the floor, now
totally useless. Giving hearty congratulations, I dropped back
down into the driver's seat.

That was one down, how many more were to follow?

We'd delivered the first blow, our message was sent. How
would they reply?

It didn't take long to find out.

Through my small opening, I could see three more of them
directly ahead a short distance away, their hands beginning to
glow bright red. Quick, strike early, I thought and One-handed
Harry seemed to read my thoughts perfectly.

BOOM!

An explosive shell was launched straight at them.

BANG!

It exploded right at their feet

Through the flash and the dust, limbs flew in all directions
leaving three gnashing heads rolling in a crater. The crater was

large enough to drive into, so I proceeded straight ahead, taking delight in the crunching I could sense coming from underneath the tracks and the moaning, mental wails that accompanied it. That was it then…chaos fell.

We'd not only attracted their attention, but also incurred their wrath as well, and it was full of fury and rage. They'd started descending on us from all sides to try and surround us. Guns spat our resentment at them. Grenades erupted with our contempt for them. The canon commanded our unwillingness to live under their heel anymore.

One of our numbers fell, Kate, lit by a firebolt. I could feel a painful and sudden loss in my head. But our firepower, with our knowledge of their weak spots combined with our improved motor-functional capability caused by the radiation had us mowing them down with wild abandon. We were firing quicker than they could raise firebolts or even get close to us. They didn't know how to counter us yet. We had the element of surprise.

There was still no sign of Muto yet. He was obviously willing to sacrifice all his pawns before making a grand entrance himself. Or perhaps he was just confident that they would sort us out without his intervention.

I kept us rolling and we soon made it to the bomb site and there it was half-buried in the middle of a main road. They'd presumably not tried to move it for fear of it exploding. I could feel the power of the radiation flowing from it. I could also feel the heat of the intense hatred of the fifty or so Supers that were stood around it, jealously guarding it and wanting to destroy anyone who came near it which was just as strong.

I definitely didn't want to risk hitting the bomb with a shell or any other part of our arsenal. Setting it off was our back-up plan. But we needed some heavy ordinance against this lot. Harry was ready, shell loaded, so I backed us away slightly thinking let them come to us. It was like a cowboy stand-off. Pete, stood on the top, in a moment of pure improvisation turned his back to them, dropped his pants showing them his bony, mouldy, smelly backside, bent over slightly and farted in their direction. Where he got the inspiration from, I didn't know, but it seemed to do the trick.

They charged – all of them.

We waited until they were almost upon us. Harry lowered the angle of the turret and canon towards the ground and then…BOOM!

Some of the Supers where caught directly in the blast as were we but our hull held.

Harry quickly reloaded.

BOOM!

We took out over half of them, recoiled the others back with the concussion and kept rattling ourselves as well. The ones on top were holding on for dear unlives.

Guns flared into action again, grenades took to the air. I pushed the levers forward and we advanced running down any of them that got in my way. Satisfying squelches and crunches came from beneath.

It was all over so quickly. The nuclear device was ours.

We could still sense hundreds of other Supers, already beginning to reform for another strike, but they were cautiously holding back, gravely aware of our firepower and determination. Not only that, they knew we were dangerous and capable of anything. For all they knew, we were just here to blow it up. It was wise not to provoke us.

Phase one complete. Now all we had to do was hold this position until Muto was found – and that was up to me. I had a personal score to settle.

This was where our team split up. Muto was mine, my own nemesis. I felt like I owed him oblivion. For what he'd done to the zombie society, for what he'd done to my family and for his overall hatred of mankind in general.

If I was going to save the humans, it had to start with the destruction of him. Only then could we make a change for the better. It was a long road to follow, but this was one mighty big step to get us underway.

I left Educated Emma in charge after parking the tank in front of the bomb as the remainder of my gang took up defensive positions. I was so proud of them, of what they'd achieved so far and the message we were delivering, and I think they all knew that. If anything was to go wrong, then Emma was to detonate the bomb and take out as many Supers as possible. Hopefully the area was deserted enough now not to create any more.

Bob suddenly decided he was coming with me. We'd been together more or less since the beginning and he wanted to support me now. Why not? The support was welcoming and, you never know, may be required against someone as strong as Muto. I felt the strong sense of comradeship between us. We looked at each other with grotesque faces and found friendship and admiration in every one of them, even though it couldn't physically be shown, we knew it.

So, I shouldered my rocket launcher, pocketed two hand guns, hooked three grenades over my shoulder on a belt and straightened up my lucky hat, still surprised that I'd managed to hold on to it all this time. Once Bob was adequately armed as well, we gave our farewells, turned our backs on our friends and set off in the direction of Muto Towers.

We'd got about half a mile down the road when the sound of gunfire began behind us.

We quickened our step.

The skyscraper loomed up before us. It was amazing how this monument to human architecture, engineering and ingenuity had survived the onslaught of the destruction relatively unscathed. The shiny glass surface did, however, manage to reflect the apocalyptic scene outside perfectly. Derelict cars with flat tyres, abandoned, covered in dust. Shop windows smashed with all their wares taken, even the electrical ones which made no sense at all, what was the point of them now? Good luck watching your new plasma screen with no electric and furthermore, no-one to broadcast anything. I wondered if the human government was still broadcasting the emergency warning. I wonder if any human government survived. If we come out of this, they may be the people to seek out if we're to have long term peaceful accord.

The top floor windows appeared to glow a lovely shade of crimson red, a bit like a sunset, though not as beautiful as you might think. I guessed Muto was angry.

What was that? Glass shattered, scattering everywhere. A few bits seemed to have lodged in my head and shoulders so I knew it must have come from above. Either that or I have the sharpest dandruff ever.

What was that big shadow?

No way – he never did?

THUD.

CRACK.

That must have been thirty stories at least, Muto was a nutter. So, that was it.

We'd finally met and there he was, stood in the centre of the concrete crater he'd just formed as he'd landed after jumping down from his penthouse apartment, no worse for the experience.

He'd hardly rotted at all. A bit grey and the clouded eyes were a giveaway, otherwise hardly changed. But he was huge, six foot eight at least and he must have been made from metal, there was no damage on him at all from the fall. He was wearing a very tidy uniform. He was definitely a soldier. Oh, shit!

I couldn't understand why he wasn't doing anything? He was just staring at us, grinning at us, his eyes glowing red. Then his hands were glowing.

Open fire!

Bob was soon letting fly with semi-automatic assault rifle and getting in some good shots, hitting Muto pretty hard. I started

unloading both my handguns, giving him all I've got. Our
ammo had done nothing, even the head shots seem to glance off
him making only tiny marks on his grey, lifeless skin.
He just continued to stand there grinning. Stood so still. His
mouth couldn't have got any wider. It's almost as if he was -
charging up!
We needed something stronger, quick – grenades. Pin, wait,
throw…
BANG.
Shit, that had hit him right in his head and he was still standing
without a care or a scratch on his skin although I appeared to
have knocked a few teeth out of that grin which, only now, he
didn't look too happy about. Who'd have guessed the ruling
overlord would be so vain?
Oh no, he'd raised his arms.
No.
FLASH.
SIZZLE.
I was still here. Still here. But why had everything turned ninety
degrees sideways? Where were my legs? Where was Bob? Oh,
there, that small pile of ash. Sorry buddy.
That was when I saw the big pair of feet in front of me. Were
they mine? They couldn't be, they were still moving towards
my head. Alright, there was no need to kick me that hard when I
was down, weren't you happy with that? I guessed not, you
sadistic bastard. I could only see the sky above me now whilst I
was laid on my back, so where was he?
Leering over me that was where, a big gap-toothed grin, man he
was looked psychotic.
What did I have in my hand? Oh, yes, something that might do
the trick, especially at this range.
What? Die? I am already dead you idiot. Go on, you just keep
gloating, I'll give you something to laugh about.
Here, taste this…
CLICK…

The End

It was at this time that I realised something quite important and was it quite some folly on my part. It was too dark, we couldn't see a thing. I walked face first into a branch.

The evergreen trees were so closely packed together, even the moonlight couldn't force its way through. Luckily this was a managed forest, so they were all purposely planted and grew in relatively uniform straight rows.

So, holding on to one another's hands we groped blindly through the forest hoping to at least reach a clearing of some sort, all the time keeping a line of trees to our right, just so we could get our bearings.

My son abruptly fell and my wife collapsed in a heap on top of him with a yelp.

'Sshh, they'll hear us!'

Obviously, they knew we were in here anyway, they'd followed us in. The brief shock of the explosive fireball wouldn't have lasted long. The gentle breeze that whispered its way through the branches carried with it those fear inducing moans of despair that never seemed to stop, like a throbbing headache. I didn't even know how they were tracking us. Could they see in the dark? Or have extra sensitive hearing? Or did they have some extra sense that they had developed in their condition? I hadn't encountered any of these in my research. However they were doing it, they were getting closer. Whatever it was, we were at a major disadvantage.

Our breaths were coming in short ragged gasps. We couldn't carry on like this forever, our bodies wouldn't let us. We were exhausted, thirsty, hungry and scared, we needed a break. The only problem was they didn't. They were unrelenting, they never stopped. It was becoming a waiting game of cat and mouse, but with several hundred cats.

When entering the forest, I was sure we'd set off in the right direction, roughly eastwards, heading for the stream that cut through the woods and that we would be able to follow uphill towards the mountains. From there, I believed we could scramble up the cliffs to some relative safety beyond their reach. But right now, I couldn't tell where we were going. We were following a straight line, but it might not even be in the right direction.

I quickly realised with fright that the moaning seemed to be coming from all sides now. Well, with the exception of one direction. Were they herding us? If not, they were surrounding us. Either way, if we didn't get a move on, we would be trapped and by the sound of it we had little choice in which direction we wanted to go. It was just so hard to tell, the trees were playing tricks with the sound.

My son started crying again.

'Son, son,' I whispered, 'be brave. I'll get you out of here, I promise.'

With a sniff, I felt his hand tighten around mine.

We carried on stumbling towards the only route I could discern that didn't have any noise coming from it when I glimpsed a light ahead.

Moonlight.

Shining on…yes…rocks.

At last, the cliff. I couldn't believe my luck. We were nowhere near the stream but somehow God was smiling on us tonight and there in the sky was his skewed silvery smile.

With the ceaseless moaning snare still tightening around us, I pulled my family towards the light as fast as I could. Puffing and panting we exploded from the forest fringe and reached the base of the rock face. It loomed up before us, almost as menacing as the threat from behind. At this point of the rock face it was very craggy; there were plenty of hand and footholds in the cold, silver looking rocks. No vegetation had taken any purchase here. This was just as well as, on our swift exit from the house; we'd had no time to bring any ropes or climbing equipment at all. As a family, we'd often done plenty of outward bound activities, climbing among them, so I was fairly confident we could reach the top.

'I'll go first to find the route, you follow me, son, and then you can come up the rear, sweetheart. Ok? We can do it. Slow and steady, we'll be up in no time.'

'Ok.' My wife exhaled very quietly, as if she'd given up. Her body looked drained of all energy and her face looked as pale as the stone around us, a perfect match for the moon.

With the groaning fast approaching and getting louder, I picked my first handhold and foothold and began to climb. A few seconds later, a bit more tentatively, my son followed. I looked down expecting to see my wife follow suit and it was then that I saw the first one appear.

From the periphery of the forest, two outstretched arms were suddenly illuminated, followed by a staggering humanoid figure.

It started lurching towards my wife. She was concentrating on my son.

'Look out! Behind you!' I shouted.

She turned and froze.

'Climb, love, climb!'

In a panic, she turned and started scrabbling up the cliff face clumsily grabbing and skidding on the rock like a dog on a tiled floor. She must have had sweaty palms as her grip kept slipping. I could do nothing; I was too high up by this point and wouldn't get to her in time before the thing reached her.

Suddenly, she screamed. A wail so full of fear and terror it cut through me like an ice blade.

It had grabbed her ankle.

Next, she was tumbling and hitting the floor heavily with a sickening thud and something cracked.

The undead thing leapt on her in an instant. Even from up here I could hear the tearing of flesh through her gasps, screams and struggles as it bit into her over and over like a rabid animal.

The screaming stopped as abruptly as it started.

'Mum?' my son whimpered.

'Sweetheart?' I mumbled.

More of the undead were emerging from the forest fringe now.

'Mum!' Desperation.

There was no answer.

'Dad, help mum. Dad…dad…da…argh!'

My son lost his grip and went skidding down amongst the rocks and stones, landing heavily with a thump. His fingers were bleeding from trying to grab sharp, jagged handholds on the way down. His body remained motionless.

I swear, my heart momentarily stopped.

I gagged.

A slight movement and a sigh. He was still alive!

Maniacally, I scrambled down as rapidly as I could but the monsters had already reached and descended on him.

Sickening wet ripping and tearing sounds came from beneath the mass of undead evil with gurgles and grunts.

My mind cracked.

Still several metres high I jumped…straight into the middle of them, landing on a mat of soft and squishy parts alike. The acrid smell hit me like a sledgehammer and I started gagging. My chest tightened, my lungs were heaving for air. I swung wildly, hitting mouldy flesh, fighting them off, but they just kept coming.

My son was so close, within reach, but I just couldn't get to him through the necrotic wall.

Pure adrenaline was pumping through my system and I didn't feel the stings of tooth on skin and the scratches of nails that were puncturing me all over. I was now on the floor, the dead weight pressing down on me...

Then...

Without warning...

They stopped...

And left us...

Laid on the floor.

We were three lumps of bleeding skin and bone, the former remains of human beings. I didn't know how I remained conscious; the rest of my body had given up. We'd soon bleed to death.

I was overwhelmed with guilt as I'd failed my family, anger as I was powerless to stop them, fear of death and numbness with the injuries inflicted upon me. I rolled over and looked straight into my wife's eyes. The pain and accusation in them struck me, I'd let her down and that hurt more than any of the bites I'd received.

Was this the end?

Shuddering from cold, shock and pain, I reached into my pocket - it was still there. Zeta 16. I pulled the lid off the vial with my last remaining strength and drank some of it. Maybe, just maybe, I could survive?

I started to drag myself across the floor, clawing the needled earth, furrowing myself through the mud, towards my family, the remaining contents of the vial clutched tightly in my hand. I never made it to them...

The vial spilt on to the ground...

All went black.

Aftermath

Those final moments with Muto had become a bit of a blur now, a fog in the past of my mind's eye. I partially remember the explosion and the concussion blast; I even remember bits of scalp, skull and brains shattering all over the place. Thankfully, not mine. The memory was a sense of finality in the moment, the yearning to inflict death and the selfless willingness to sacrifice myself for the cause.

I never expected to survive.

If surviving was what you could call this current condition I was experiencing. Of course, I'd not fully escaped the blast as the rocket hit Muto at point blank in the face. It had taken something as radical as that to even finish him off. I'd suffered major superficial damage (superficial in the zombie sense), by losing most of the skin on the left-hand side of my body, my left eye, my left ear and most of my nose. Not forgetting I'd lost my legs from Muto's fire bolt, so it might take me a bit longer to get around from now on. Perhaps they could call me butt-drag or something like that now? They'd love that. But when push came to shove, at least I was still un-alive.

Laying there on the tarmac under the former Muto towers, covered in Muto gore and entrails that were mixing with my own, I was feeling a sense of tremendous achievement. We'd done it.

I'd done it.

Muto was gone. Surely all the other Supers would now see what us 'normals' were capable and see that we needed to restore some sort of order. Otherwise they'd be sorry. I hoped there wasn't another one just waiting to take Muto's place, I didn't fancy going through all this again.

More importantly, zombie-kind, of which there were probably billions of us now, might now listen to our message – we needed to live in peace, firstly, with ourselves, but more importantly, with the humans.

Through the blurry vision of my right eye, I captured a shadowy movement, a collection of shadows, in fact, with footsteps and a strange, squeaky, rattling sound accompanying them. I feared this would be the retribution coming my way for taking out their glorious leader.

As they got closer, there was relief as I recognised the silhouettes although I was sad not to see that many of them. Leading the way, pushing a wheelchair, was Educated Emma and behind her was Harry and Jane, and Pete brought up the rear. With them, came two Supers, heads bowed in submission under the careful watch of Pete's gun, but no other expression on their undead faces from what I could see. Their shoulders carried the weight of defeat.

You're right; I do look a bit rough. Oh I see, they've surrendered. Good. They felt Muto's mental hold disappear and felt they'd been released? Really? He must have had a powerful hold over them. I'm sure they are sorry. If they really mean it, they will have to come over to our cause, we can't have any more rogue Supers trying to dictate over everyone again.

Now stop staring at me and pick me up will you? I'm tired of looking at your shins.

As they gently lifted me to make sure nothing else fell off, they carefully placed me in a wheelchair, which turned out to be the origin of the strange noise I'd heard, and strapped me in with a bit of rope. I tested my arms and neck for any movement and there was barely any response. Once again, now more than ever, I found myself thankful that I couldn't feel any pain. Then an idea struck me.

I instructed them to push me to the bomb site hoping that a good dose of radiation might just help with a bit of a patching up job. If it had the power to restore us before, I hoped it might just help me get back into some sort of working condition. I did not want to be pushed around for the rest of my days.

Having come this far now, I was determined to see my mission through. Our next step was to contact and confront humans. If we were going to treat with them, I needed to be in some sort working order to get me through. There was no way I'd be left out of that encounter.

As I was pushed through the remains of the city, I consulted with Emma. They'd barely been able to hold off the oncoming Supers as they defended the bomb until the moment that Muto was destroyed. In the moments of confusion that overtook them, Emma had taken control of the situation (with a few well placed shells) and brought them to order. They seemed to lose their willingness to fight once their leader's mental hold had let them go. She was relieved that she didn't have to set off the bomb as that would have meant we failed.

As we talked further, we agreed that this place would be a great place to start again. If we could attract our fellow zombies here, we could educate them with our new found values and ethics as well as regenerate some of our less able contingent bringing about a working population again.

Humans would never be able to survive here with this amount of radioactivity, so this could be somewhere out of their way where we wouldn't bother them, we could protect them against this area.

As we got closer to the device, that strange tingle enveloped what was left of my body but was much stronger now and I could sense some motor function returning to my battered limbs although I was pretty sure I would need to spend a long time here to benefit from a proper recovery. It also wasn't going to bring my legs back, so it looked like I was going to be stuck in this wheelchair from now on. That may make life a bit tricky, but hey, it could be worse. My memory drifted back to my wife in the pit and I counted how lucky I was. As a doctor I'd met plenty of disabled people in my before life and had always been inspired by how they lived. I could do that too. I was still in better condition than some of my zombie kind unbelievably. At least I wasn't like Post-top Carl.

By now, we'd got to the bomb and it struck me how well Emma and the gang had done in holding onto it. Scattered in piles were the headless and dismembered bodies of dozens of Supers. To my remorse, I could also see the splattered remnants of Kate still on top of the tank. I decided there and then that we should raise some sort of memorial to the fallen members of my cohort, all of them, for their bravery, their compassion and their sacrifice to the cause. I realised I would never have got this far without them and it was now, more than ever, that I wished I was able to express my own feelings and emotions more humanly. I knew I wanted to cry for them, mourn them, my brain told me so. But in to my inherited state, the best I could do was keep remembering them. As heroes. It didn't seem enough, but it would have to be. I now wished I'd known their real names, more about their lives before, but as was our curse that was never meant to be.

I looked around at the remaining rag-tag band around me now. They had started to congregate in a circle. I could hear what they wanted, what they needed. The released Supers were confused, looking for direction. The remains of my gang wanted to know what we were going to do next. They all looked at me with blank-faced expectation in their eyes. The first sign of life I had ever seen in these undead bodies. I hadn't realised how much they'd come to rely on me. Now that we had reached our goal, there was a sense of unknowing ahead of them and they looked to me to fill that gap as I had done before. I needed to teach them some independence.

I knew I should say something important, something poignant, something epic, but my weary brain was unable to bring such words to the fore, so I relayed one simple message to them all... Thank-you all. We are going to begin again.

Sanctuary

Things had been going pretty well so far since that fateful day when we'd descended the ridge. The nuclear device had regenerated the majority of what was left of me, allowing me to move around in my wheelchair, albeit slowly, using my own arms. I'm still not sure where Emma managed to find it, but I was grateful that she did. If there was somewhere I couldn't access, with steps or rubble and so on, I had now inherited two new willing assistants to help me. Both of them were former Supers so ashamed by their actions and the actions of Muto that they were eager to make up for their crimes in some way and thought they could do this by supporting me directly (almost literally sometimes) as the new leader who had a moral code and acting upon my every whim. It seemed they still needed direct guidance, something I found was apparent in a lot of the freed subjects. I wasn't too comfortable with this, bearing in mind the demise of their previous master, but they insisted, so I treated them as friends and colleagues, not subordinates, and gave them a few responsibilities to help me out. I even gave them names, which I think they were more pleased with as formerly they were referred to as Runt and Smash and they didn't like the negative connotation that went with them. Firstly, Tiny, who stood at six foot three, became my liaison to the newly liberated Supers. As the zombie mutants returned from scouting missions that Muto had sent them on, I needed someone to help integrate them into our new society and instil the new values into them without them going nuts and trying to destroy everything. Obviously, during their ventures, they were unaware of what had happened here although they all sensed Muto's absence on their return.

Tiny was very good at this, especially with the ones who were resistant as it seemed he didn't have any morals when it came to vaporising their heads with a fire bolt should they fail to comply. This was still a bit worrying, but I knew Tiny had the right meaning behind his actions. He'd really hated what he'd been and couldn't bare to see anything like that continue. Especially with the vicious Supers, who had been under Muto's heel for so long, all they knew was violence, anger and the want to do harm. Tiny really abhorred that now.

My other assistant, Skinny, was surprisingly a very well organised individual, probably a civil servant in his former life, and became my right-hand man for welcoming wandering zombies into our new collective working very closely with Emma. He would make sure they had their needs met, got them some exposure to the bomb for regeneration, a place to stay and rehydrate and organised a census, giving every single zombie a name. This was so we could begin to get a democracy going like we used to have in the days before Muto's dictatorship, but to make it fairer we knew everyone had to be recognised. It was excellent that we found a baby name book in an abandoned apartment, that made things so much easier. I think it was the simple act of giving all our new citizens a name that made the newcomers feel like they were really part of something special and a feeling of worth and belonging, even if some of them only had a simple understanding of such things. It took some of them back to the days when unlife had some meaning. Names also made it possible for relationships to be formed. Not romantically, of course, no-one ever wants to imagine a couple of zombies doing the bedroom jig, how sickening, but to make friendships.

Skinny also arranged for scouts and patrols of volunteers to bring in our wayward brothers and sisters and establish a sort of 'police force' to stop any sieges upon human compounds or stop any more murdering or further human conversions. This was also rather difficult at first as at any one time there were often several thousand congregated together, still following the old ways. I was told the look on the humans' faces was a sight to behold as a group of fairly agile zombies would appear and escort the moaning, drooling, limping, rotting ones away to leave them alone. Especially when the commander of the round-up expedition would give the humans a friendly wave and a nod goodbye as they disappeared over the horizon. I really wished I could be there to see it, to be back on the frontline, not conquering and destroying, but giving gestures of goodwill to the human survivors in complete contrast to the old days. Eventually our territory would have to expand as eventually I expected to bring back millions of zombies and they couldn't all be housed here. I was so glad we didn't have to feed and dress them as well, that would have been impossible.

Hopefully, by now, the humans were beginning to recognise these strange occurrences as attempts at peaceful relations with the withdrawal of our kind from their lands, a sign that they could start to feel safe. I'd come to decision that it might be time to test that theory.

I was currently sat in my wheelchair and looking down on the cityscape below from one of the skyscrapers I'd taken for our 'base of operations'. It was a term I still didn't like, it was too military, but it worked. I could see (and hear) all sorts of things going on from up here and it helped me to concentrate and coordinate them. I knew that soon I needed to form some sort of council or government of elected officials but that wasn't viable just yet until we had our list of registered voters and enough individuals in the city to take on these roles of responsibility as leaders and counsellors. So for now, I was in temporary charge of the rebuilding with my trusted team behind me. My mental ability, the very thing that had won us our freedom, had trapped me in this position. But I always knew this would be that case, so I just had to get on with it.

I was watching some groups of organised zombies starting to tidy up the city, voluntarily of course, taking some pride in their new home, when it struck me. I knew the individual for the job, the one who could lead, my own shadow – Educated Emma. I'd put her in charge of the education and rehabilitation program helping our new undead fit into their new situation; give them a feeling of worth and a new purpose in unlife in our new city. She'd done a terrific job so far as my number two. The evidence of that was working below me right now. I knew she was still plagued by those memories of Mungo in the school and knew she would never let such a thing happen again. So who better to take control and educate our new members, instilling them with the values and ethics of the revolution than her?

Just as if she knew I was thinking about her, which she probably did, she appeared through the door and entered the meeting room. She'd regenerated remarkably well and was looking quite smart in a new grey trouser suit and blouse combo with some smart, black leather boots she'd acquired from one the department stores. Stilettos were obviously a no-no, not with our shaky balance, but I believe she could have carried them off if she'd wanted to. Emma believed that we should start taking care of our appearance should we ever come into human contact, which was an excellent idea. It might give them more reason to trust us if we looked a bit more civilised and not like a dirty, raggedy, blood-thirsty mob. If it wasn't for the grey, lifeless skin, cloudy eyes, the missing hair, the exposed tendons in her hand and the battle gouges across her face, you'd never know she was a zombie.

I started to put forward my thoughts to her about me approaching a human colony and starting a dialogue with them. As anticipated, Emma was apprehensive about me going, she was a little overprotective of me in my 'wheeled' condition and perhaps a little apprehensive of losing my leadership ability as well, but thankfully, after I'd listed all the pros and cons, she could see my logic. She even agreed to come with me as well as develop some communication as a way to get our message across.

I instructed Tiny to advise us of any human groups he found on any of his scheduled scouting missions that he thought might be approachable and open to us contacting them.

A couple of days had gone by and Tiny reported back to us that there was a reasonably large band of humans on the coast, about five days east of our position that may be suitable for our diplomatic envoy. They'd been living on boats and raiding the coastline, reminiscent of something I'd seen before, but they weren't organised in the military sense, they were likely civilians, so we may be able to approach them more safely. Knowing we'd never be able to communicate with them verbally or telepathically, Emma and I had been starting to develop a way we might talk to them through signs and gestures. I'd found that I was still able to write, but many of my colleagues hadn't retained this skill, so we concocted a rudimentary form of gesturing sign language that we hoped would get us close enough to allow me to use writing to 'talk' further. Something similar had worked with the survivors on the mountain so we were willing to give it another try. It was as simple as palm face out for 'stop', waving for 'hello', hand held out available for shaking showed we wanted to be friends. By tapping our mouths with fingers, we hoped showed we wanted to talk to them and cupping our ears (if we still had them) showed we wanted to listen, and so it went on. It was like going on holiday to a foreign country and trying to get your message across when you didn't know the language. We had developed other terms as well and Emma was going to put them in to her education program for our scouting teams who may encounter other human colonies on their patrols.

I'd decided to take only a small group on this diplomatic mission, just in case anything bad might happen like gunfire, grenades flamethrowers and all the usual stuff we came to expect. I also decided I wouldn't take Tiny, Skinny or Emma with me as they'd become too important in our new cultural system. They would have to carry on in my absence; they were the ones I trusted to see the job through should anything happen to me.

I needed other people I could trust though, so who better than the survivors of the city assault from my gang, Harry and Peter. A few days later, we all acquired new clothes, shoes and hats, anything to cover the grisly bits, and even some sunglasses, which I had to stick on with tape due to the lack of ears, and we looked pretty damn smart. Better than being held together by rags and tight Lycra anyway, I still can't believe I used to wear that. Once we'd gathered together, I instructed there was no time like the present, so, right there and then, we set off east with the directions Tiny had given us, looking to meet us some humans and let diplomacy begin.

First Contact

The time was upon us.

The crossroads to the future.

If I could have felt fear, I think I would have been more afraid now than I had when I was facing Muto.

Thankfully, my body still didn't respond to stress and anxiety because if it did, then I'm pretty sure my heart would have burst out of my chest and exploded.

After five days of walking, or rolling in my case as I couldn't drive anymore with no legs, we'd come upon the human settlement as described by Tiny. It was night-time now and beyond the edge of the quaint, dilapidated harbour village we could see the faint lights bobbing on the sea like dancing angels with reflections twinkling on the gentle waves that the boats sat safely upon. I had no doubt there would be members of my kind under the water staring up at them with only one thought in their heads – we want brains, get down here. There was a remarkable amount of my kind that had ended up underwater. It was a bit difficult to get back up when you don't float. We usually had to wait for a current to take us and wash us back to shore, unless we found our way there first. It would probably have freaked the humans out to know that, but I guess ignorance is bliss. Before I'd left, Emma and Tiny had set up coast line and shore parties just to watch for any zombie emerging from bodies of water.

Anyway, I knew the humans would have to come ashore at some point, if only to replenish their fresh water stores as they couldn't take water from the sea. There was evidence here that they used this port frequently so it was a case of waiting. Therefore we took the opportunity to take a look around as none of us needed the light to see. These humans had been quite ingenious. They had set up vegetable and fruit allotments close to their landing point on any piece of land they could find, verges, gardens, even roundabouts, near to a stream inlet that flowed to the sea. They set up barrels, buckets, anything that could capture rain water to make sure that they didn't drink any contaminated water. This was all defended with well built, reinforced large metal fences to keep out predators, animal and zombie alike.

I was relieved they'd managed find a way to survive but they obviously still knew they weren't safe, with plenty of our number roaming about. It was best that they stayed on the water, out of reach.

Tiny had informed me that his scouts had picked up most of our rogues from this area and escorted them back to the city so they shouldn't have seen one of my kind for days, not in large numbers anyway. I assumed they would notice us once daylight arrived unless they had night-vision goggles; hopefully they had some wits about them. In fact, I was counting on it or this trip would be in vain.

The dawn was slowly approaching now, the sky taking on an orange hue, so I wheeled over to their landing quay closely followed by Peter and Harry to await the humans awakening or get spotted by their morning lookouts.

We looked quite dapper in our smart, expensive, fine cut cloth tailored suits. Before we'd left Peter had even found a pair of mannequin legs, dressed them in my suit trousers and attached them to my wheelchair. Totally pointless, I know. I suppose this could be taken for vanity, but I guess I didn't want to freak out the humans too much by appearing as an animated torso in a wheelchair trying to communicate with them. I guess I was using the same excuse for my stylish panama hat wanting to hide my scalp. But the truth was I just thought it looked cool. Something a visiting human diplomat might wear. It was then I wondered what happened to my lucky helmet. I think I would have felt more secure in that.

The sun suddenly burst above the horizon and we could see movement start to occur on the boats out on the sea. The nearest one was only stationed about two hundred yards offshore, not that far, but far enough. The vessels varied in size and shape from small pleasure craft to huge car ferries but they had managed to lash them all together with ropes and makeshift walkways to form a floating island community.

There was a sudden glint from one of the bridge windows of a larger craft; a telescope or binoculars no doubt catching their lenses in the sun. They probably knew we were here now. There was sudden, frantic action among a few of the decks and in no time, two small inflatable dinghies with outboard motors were tearing across the waves towards us halting just beyond the end of the quay, bobbing like rubber ducks. Anxious faces behind guns were looking towards their fenced off allotments and water collectors behind us.

We stood still, looking out at them trying not to make any move that looked aggressive or threatening. Normally by now, I'm sure they would have expected us to be lurching towards them. Goodness knows if it was working. These humans were looking at three smart suits inhabited by grizzled monsters, with one in a wheelchair, staring back at them. Who knows what was going through their minds?

BANG, WHIZZ, POP.

I got my answer. A bullet burst through my chest exiting through the back of my wheelchair. They'd ruined my jacket, I couldn't believe it. Then again, I guess I should have expected that.

It hadn't started well.

I instructed Peter to get out our secret weapon. He reached into his inside jacket pocket.

A few more bullets fizzed in the stones before us sending up small showers of dust and shards.

Peter pulled out a folded white cloth, unfurled it, lifted it aloft and started waving it above his head. I hoped the old fashioned gestures still held some meaning in this apocalyptic day and age. But, not only that, the fact that something considered brain-dead and dangerous was actually displaying some intelligence in knowing what this symbol meant.

At least that stopped the bullets flying.

Motors revved up again and the boats resumed their journey to the shore although a little slower and more tentative. Peter continued waving his white flag as they landed on the quay, disembarked cautiously and tied there boats in readiness for a quick getaway if required.

Now, close up, we could see the tired, confused yet anguished look on their faces. More importantly, there were a number of guns trained on us yet all aiming for our chests, they hadn't learned the proper way to kill us yet. We remained still and silent. We'd worked very hard at home to overcome all our urges to attack through self-motivation and education and we were perfect at it. But they weren't to know that.

There were six men in total, three of them with guns, powerful rifles, but one of them in particular looked to be the leader by the way the others glanced to him for movement and instruction. They halted twenty yards away and everything went silent only to be broken by the lap of the waves breaking against the harbour side. There was barely any wind and the sun showed sweat glistening on their pale, hairy faces.

The seconds ticked by like hours, which meant nothing to us but probably felt like an age to them, each side waiting for the other to make a move. I knew it would have to be me, I was prepared for that. I gripped the rims of my wheels and gradually edged forward. Guns were quickly trained and focused on me, the men chattered amongst each other barking quick rehearsed commands. I stopped and raised my hand flat in front of me showing them my palms. They recognised the gesture and relaxed their weapons slightly but still stood alert and ready. I continued my progress. I was now ten yards away so I stopped; sitting alone in front of them, vulnerable to their attack should they decide on that course of action. I displayed a massive show of trust on my part. Raising my hand to my mouth I made a gesture expressing my desire to talk and then I pointed at them before cupping my ear.

The faces I looked at were priceless, screwed up in disbelief, confusion and amazement. There were also a couple of 'O' shaped mouths. Typical, I thought, first contact with the humans and who do they send out to meet us? Their stupid grunts, that's who, that couldn't add two plus two, never mind interpret a couple of communication gestures. Amazingly, my hopes were raised briefly when one of the younger ones, who must have been about sixteen by the pathetically wispy bum-fluff on his face, showed a spark of acknowledgment and blurted out...

'You want to talk and us to listen?'

Eureka! First contact made, even if it was with a spotty docile teenager. I nodded with as much enthusiasm I could muster knowing I couldn't show any emotion on my withered, burned unresponsive face. The youth looked pleased with himself before being reminded of the situation he was in by one of the older, more senior members of the party, with a grunt. His head dropped slightly, rebuffed.

'You've got to be joking!' one of the other men commented. 'Is this some kind of stitch up? Kev? Is this your doing? Where are you? Come on out!'

I shook my head from side to side emphatically. Please understand we need to talk. I did the mouth gesture again.

'It's trying to say something,' said the lead man looking rough with deep bags under his eyes, a bushy beard flecked with grey, sallow skin and stained dirty clothes. His chronological age was probably about thirty but he looked about fifty. 'Well, bugger me; one of these murderous bastards actually wants to talk. Yeah, right! It's a shame you didn't want to talk whilst you were ripping my brother's throat and chewing on his brains, did you? You disgusting, rotten arseholes...' The gun came up again and another two bullets punctured my ribcage and lungs.

I sat stoically, taking the abuse. I guess in some way, I had expected this. Devoid of our extreme emotions, we progressed quite logically these days, but humans were still over-emotional creatures. I think I'd have done something similar in his position should zombies have done anything to my family when I had survived to watch them suffer. He was allowably furious. I raised my hands above my head in submission. Somehow, I think that helped. He obviously needed to get this out of his system, to feel he had control over us. But seeing that I could still move, he backed down slightly and let out a sigh.

I pulled out the whiteboard and dry-wipe marker pen that I had tucked down by the side of me on the wheelchair and held it up to show them that I had nothing nasty that could hurt them, then I proceeded to write something down whilst all the time I had six anxious, yet fascinated, faces concentrating intently on my every move.

Please don't do that, it tickles, I wrote and showed it to him.

The lead guy's face was stunned; his mouth again in a massive O. Silence fell again for a moment and then was suddenly swept away by his sudden guffaws of laughter.

'Ha…ha…I…don't…believe…hoo…it…hoo…this…dead…thi ng's…risen… up…ha…ha…with a flaming…ho…ho…sense of bloody humour!'

The others took this as an invitation to join in and the tension visibly lifted. I wished I could have joined in too, but squeezing my lungs to inhale and exhale the air through my ragged voice box might have grossed them out a bit, even if it was my favourite party trick.

After a few minutes of calming down he said, 'Ok, ugly, you wanted to talk – so talk. What do you want to say?'

Peace. We want peace.

'Stop trying to kill us then.'

We will. We've changed. We want to help.

'Jonny, better go and get the council members. I'm pretty sure they are going to want to get involved here.' He made a brief gesture with his hand towards the boat.

'Yes, boss.' The young lad got into one of the boats and sped off back to the flotilla. The other men had now relaxed and had dropped their guns to their sides.

Thank-you.

'Don't thank me yet, ugly, they might want to torch you as soon as they see you, even if you do look ridiculous in that hat and that wheelchair.'

We try!

He humphed and looked like he was getting used to the idea of talking with us. His posture had become much more relaxed, seemingly confident that he was safe. There didn't seem to be any harm that could come from a crippled zombie. Lucky it was me though and not one of my super-mutant deranged brothers or sisters. That could still have turned out a bit nasty. Don't need agility when a fire bolt will do the trick.

Before long, the youth had returned and the humans' council was stood with us on the quayside. Peter and Harry were still backed off at a respectable distance, not wanting to agitate these newcomers, and allowed me to build up their trust. There were three men and three women, all in their fifties or sixties by my guess, but they looked just as bedraggled as the other six men not to mention the drawn, bag-eyed look on their pale, grey faces. They carried with them an air of importance, yet looked slightly slumped with the weight of responsibility on their shoulders. I remembered that times must be so hard and desperate for these people almost so close to being obliterated by my kind and now, here I was, knocking on their front door wanting to be friends with them. One of their most hated enemies. The whole situation sounded surreal. In fact, it was preposterous. What was I thinking?

Jonny must have apprised them of the situation on the boat journey across as they seemed ready to talk. When I say talk, I think I meant ask a lot of questions.

'So, what do they call you?' one short, slim, bald councilmen asked. 'It may help us to trust you if we told us what you were called.'

My mind blanked. I hadn't anticipated that. As hard as I tried to remember my name, my human name, had never come back to me, even now. So I just told them what Tiny and Skinny had started calling me...

Willie Wheels, I wrote.

'Really?' he smirked glancing at the wheelchair. 'Willie? Ok then, Mr Wheels, well I'm Mr Suggs. Tell us why you're here then?' He was direct, I gave him that.

It took a long time writing down everything I needed to get across, good job I couldn't cramp or my fingers would have gone numb, but in all fairness, they read everything I wrote with unreadable expressions on their faces. You could tell they were trying to come to terms with a literate zombie. If I was getting through to them, I could not tell. I just kept going. After a considerable length of time, they were beginning to look weary. I wondered if I should have a moan and quickly gnash my teeth just to liven things up a bit, as a joke, but I was pretty sure that would be a mistake. Of course, they were bound to get tired. After all, they didn't possess our infinite stamina and had more than likely had anything near a proper meal in a long time. The sun was now high in the sky right above us, so I must have been scribing for hours. It looked like we had come far enough for now, they needed a break.

Enough for now?

'That's a lot to think about Mr Wheels,' Mr Suggs said rubbing his eyes and letting out a big sigh. 'We'll have to discuss this back on board with the masses. If what you're telling us is true, the whole zombie society thing, it's going to take a lot to convince us all. You've been ravaging and murdering us for such a long time, you've decimated our population, done barbaric, despicable and unholy things to us and now you approach us and say 'I want peace' like it's the most casual request in the world. It all seems a bit farfetched to me. But, I can tell you're different, there is something about you. I have to admit, I thought you were all mindless killers, never once did I think you had intelligence. Bit of a shock that. I guess that makes you even more dangerous than we thought. But you have also put us in another awkward position, what if we don't want peace? What if we want to wipe you out? Exact our revenge on you? Could we now do that with a clear conscience? Knowing you were sentient and offering an olive branch. Then again, you could roll over us with your sheer numbers and wait us out. What sort of future is that for our kids?' He rubbed his eyes with the heels of his palms.

I just sat and nodded solemnly through his whole speech. I could see his turmoil. 'Come back tomorrow, Mr Wheels, we'll see what my people think. Don't think I don't recognise your bravery in coming to us. Let's just hope something happens for the best, eh?'

Thank-you Mr Suggs, you're very fair.

With that, the humans got back into their small boats and cruised back to their floating village leaving me alone on the quayside. Even the waves had quietened in the gravity of the moment.

I replayed Mr Suggs' last words in my head. Had I detected a bit of hope in what he said? Or was that just my hopeless optimism? I went back up to where Harry and Peter were still stood patiently waiting for me, and filled them in on the events of the meeting. They gave an enthusiastic response, but I'm not sure they really understood everything that had taken place. If only I could restore others' memories to the comprehension that I now enjoyed. We had the rest of the day and all night to wait, if we were lucky, before we saw them again, but that meant nothing to us. We could feel the eyes from the boats watching, examining us, but perhaps now they were looking at us a little differently.

<u>The Beginning</u>

It was dark.

It was quiet.

Absence of light? I couldn't tell. Either way it was a blackout.

I was in a forest, I think.

The stings of the bites had worn off, I couldn't feel anything. Worryingly, I felt nothing at all. My body was numb. No warm, no cold, couldn't feel the ground under me, couldn't even feel it when I touched myself. Rubbing my hands over my body, I barely even registered the touch in my fingers or my heavily punctured skin.

But I was moving. I was moving but not feeling? How could that be?

My other senses were working and eventually I realised my eyes were closed. So I tentatively opened them and looked down at my body. To my surprise, I could see perfectly, clear as day. But wasn't it still night? Wasn't that the moon I could see through that clearing? I was surrounded by pine trees on most that I could see disappearing into the distance and had a cliff face behind me. The rags of my clothes clung to my body, plastered to my skin with mud, dried blood and saliva.

So much blood! Why wasn't I bleeding now? So many wounds, I should have bled to death.

What had happened? How did I get here?

My memory was blank. I knew I was in a forest, but that's all that I knew. I started to panic. Well, at least I thought I was panicking. My mind was confused, dizzy and unable to think coherently, yet the rest of me wasn't reacting as I would have expected when anxiety takes over. No sweating, no cramps, no loss of breath, no increased heartbeat…wait, no heartbeat at all! I instinctively grasped at my chest, hoping to feel…anything.

Nothing. Was I dead?

I couldn't even hear a thump in my ears of a pulse pumping blood to my brain.

I wasn't even breathing yet I wanted to scream.

I came over very peculiar.

Something wasn't right.

I tried to stand up. My clothes cracked as I moved. My body was answering my mental commands but the response I got wasn't exactly what I'd expected. I reacted jerkily, slowly, as if I was rising and learning to walk all over again. But I wasn't exerting any effort, I felt…automated.

After a few attempts, I was finally on my feet. It took all my concentration to even move, my brain almost didn't seem capable of processing more than one thing at once. I stood for a few moments, gently swaying, finding my equilibrium.

Then, I felt the burning.

A cold storm raged through my body like electrocution multiplied by ten. I felt like I should cramp up and fight it but my body wouldn't react. I just stood there; the mental anguish I suffered was the only way the pain would register.

Eventually, after what seemed an eternity, it relented and I was left with just a feint itching, only just detectable on the edge of my senses as though hovering on the outskirts of my physical form. It was quite unnerving.

Then, there, just a few yards away, were two other figures. They too were jerkily, lurching about similar to myself. Did they look familiar? I was having difficulty focussing on any coherent thoughts beyond the here and now and I couldn't seem to form any connection as to who they were. One was a smaller version of me, I could see the similarities. The other was different in shape and had lumps and curves in different places. Both were in a similar condition to me. Covered in grime, blood and ragged clothes. We'd all obviously suffered the same incident. Why were they here?

I could hear footsteps approaching, lots of them, from the trees, and then there they were, dozens of other figures, similar to the three of us here. Their faces were masks of horror, totally inanimate. Yet…they were communicating.

Yes, I replied, I will come with you. I understand there is nothing to fear. Thank-you for your welcome.

The other two were coming as well.

Where are we going? Oh, the city. We'll be told more when we get there. Some sort of training, eh? We'd be a welcome addition to society. Really? Ok.

Well, we are all so alike; I guess I must trust them. I do sense a strange belonging, as if we all should be together as one. During this uncertain time, it felt quite comforting. They seem quite friendly. I feel like I'm floating along. The other two are looking at me. I wonder if I'm familiar to them?

We've got a long walk ahead of us? Ok, I suppose that will give me time to think. Although, that function seems to be getting harder and harder. I'll guess I'll just follow, for now.

I hope my memory comes back soon.

Epilogue

It had been six months now. Six months since that fateful day when I had rolled up to the humans on the quayside of that old quiet fishing village asking for peace.
So far, we'd struck up a good accord with them. We helped them out with rebuilding their lives and they help us mutually. A trust has formed, a fragile one, but a trust all the same.
Instead of killing one another, we save one another. If we find any wandering humans, once we've stopped the shooting, attacking or running away, we pointed or escorted them in the direction of the nearest safe haven and if rogue zombies start wandering into human territory, we have an undead diplomatic service (like zombie body guards) staying close to the human colonies that then bring them back to our city for re-education. Yes, they're allowing zombies to stay with them. If that isn't trust, I don't know what is, even if it's still, for the moment, still a fragile one.
The newly elected council of undead has been formed, and I'm pleased that Emma, Tiny and Skinny were all elected, Emma as Prime Minister, Tiny as Foreign Secretary and Skinny as Home Secretary. They would do a great job, I almost felt like a proud father.
But me? Why wasn't I elected?
I'd had enough of leading for a while; I needed a rest, not physically of course, mentally. I needed a holiday, some time to reflect. It was hard having a functioning brain in a body that just doesn't respond adequately enough and with so much memory recall that I still had to come to terms with. It was like being in a cage and swimming through treacle. I had a new respect for disabled people now in the time before. But after all that had taken place, the revolution, that battle, the society reintegration and the peace negotiations, I was mentally exhausted.

So, I'd decided I'd go on a vacation. Yep, a holiday, a break from it all and why not? Had I not deserved it?

I'd roped in a 'younger' looking zombie friend, Cyril he was called, one with all his faculties still intact and a keenness to explore beyond the city boundaries, as my aide. In a flash of inspiration I taught him how to drive. Or was it madness? I was quite lucky to survive that episode, it was a good job we can take some damage and have no nerves, but we got there eventually.

As a gift, the humans were kind enough to give us a still working truck and some petrol. When asked by Cyril where I wanted to go, I just pointed out the large forested mountains in the distance and the road that led towards it. Somewhere far away and remote, I instructed, where I couldn't hear everyone's voice in my head all the time.

It was a pleasant drive, the leaves were wearing their autumn hues and the nights were gradually getting longer, though that still meant nothing to us. It was beautiful either night or day to me now. The humans, however, would probably start to appreciate our help as the winter drew in and supplies started to dwindle. We were great winter survivors, oblivious to the cold weather, though we still had to be careful not to get caught in ice by staying still too long in wet conditions. With limited supplies and clothes, surviving winter would be a hard task for them. But it would be easier with our help.

Cyril and I must have driven continuously for days, randomly following Cyril's rotten nose as I'd lost mine along roads that still looked accessible. We weren't in a rush. The freedom from responsibility had become quite liberating. But after a while, I began to feel like I knew where I was going, as if I was being drawn subconsciously back to somewhere I knew. Some where I knew very well. A place that was dear to me where I must have felt safe with strong feelings of home and family. I just couldn't quite recall the full details, exact route and so on, so, frustratingly, I'd just let my instinct lead the way and hoped it would take me to this unknown place that I might be yearning for. It was just a feeling of direction because the environment had let nature take over again and everything had changed so much.

We'd been casually driving up a hill totally surrounded by evergreen woodland when I glimpsed a rather non-descript gate with a track leading off into the gloom. Recognition hit me like a thunderbolt. Was this what my subconscious had been searching for? I immediately instructed Cyril to turn around (avoiding the big drop to our right as I didn't fancy going down there) and head back to the secluded gate.

The driveway, broken up and heavily overgrown with grass, weeds and other plants, wound its way up the shallow hill until there, stood before us, was a large stone Victorian country house in a clearing with a black 4x4 car parked outside, the latter now decorated with the grey of dust and the green of lichen. A big bay window commanded the front façade, but most of the glass panes had been broken inwards, as it had with most of the downstairs windows, and there was evidence of scratching and scrambling up the walls where stone had been scarred and paintwork was flaking.

I knew this place. It haunted me from some deep forgotten memory.

The car, the bay window, a vague image of someone stood there. Looking out.

Wife?

Son?

Despair?

Escape?

I was impelled to go inside.

Cyril parked up next to the 4x4, got out, and helped me into my wheelchair, though there was no chance I was entering the building in it without his help up the stairs that led to what remained of the front door which was hanging haphazardly from its hinges. Cyril made short work of the door, strapping young zombie that he was, and we tentatively made our way inside, him carrying me like a baby, avoiding the wood and glass debris that lay strewn about.

Through into the hallway, turning right, then into the lounge and there was the bay window again. A shadow of a distraught woman standing there flashed through my mind and the need to protect a scared, cowering child, a boy, came to me. On the leaf covered floor were the rotten remains and bones of a fallen zombie, the skull off to one side, picked clean by carrion eaters that had gained access. The wildlife was probably thriving without the obstruction of man.

At the foot of the stairs was a pile of broken furniture covered in brown, dried streaks, probably blood, where bare hands had been tearing through the wood and fabric, possibly trying to get at a victim upstairs. The poor souls must have barricaded themselves in. It looked like the attackers had managed to break through. Here and there were also a couple of crushed, dismembered bodies, but their faces were twitching, their heads were still animated. They were pleased to see someone had arrived.

They escaped did they? You've been here a long time; of course we'll take you back.

Cyril kindly put me down and carried the heads to the back of the truck. I imagine those two would be pleased with a change of scenery. Looking at the amount of dust they'd acquired, they must have been here for quite some time.

When he picked me up again, I guided Cyril upstairs, so he carried me on his back with my arms wrapped around his neck so I could see over his shoulder. All the furniture, beds and all, had obviously been thrown down the stairs as a makeshift barricade as all the rooms were virtually empty.

That twitching unease was still tickling my brain, I was almost certain I'd been here, but for some reason the memories I desperately wished to recall just wouldn't surface. I was frustrated yet again. Had I been one of the zombies to chase these people from their home? I could only imagine it must have been just after I'd been turned, my brain was pretty scrambled back then, a naively new zombie, maybe that's why this place was so familiar.

Then my eyes fixed on something unusual. A simple brown manila envelope pinned to the wall with 'Read Me' scrawled on it.

That was curious.

A message left by the former inhabitant perhaps? A letter from the dead? It seemed to have been deliberately put there. They must have been caught or turned or maybe even escaped because there were no corpses or skeletons here.

I felt compelled to honour this mystery writer's last request. Pulling the envelope from the wall a strange sensation touched me as if I'd touched this envelope before. Cyril then set me down on the floor to ponder this find. I opened it up to find a hand written letter…

To whoever finds this letter,
If you have survived the outbreak and have found this letter, then I offer you my congratulations as well as my sympathies. It seems you have succeeded where I have failed. I can only say I did my best. I was so close to finding the cure but it was too late to share it with the world, the plague has spread too far, and in my cowardice I have brought it with me to this remote location and it seems this is where the secret will be lost. They have found us. They are everywhere. We are trapped.
I brought my wife, Kelly, and my son, Cameron, here thinking they would be safe, yet it seems I have condemned them to a fate worse than death as those things have found us and are intent on our destruction. I must have been stupid believing I could outrun them but when a contagion spreads that fast, how can any human being hope to survive or escape? Especially when they are turned into the evil, bloodthirsty, relentless

creatures that they are? Those are the same creatures that are trying to get at us through the blocked stairway, right now. We've run out of options and all we have left is one final attempt at an escape plan. We're going to make a break for it into the mountains on the other side of the forest. If we're lucky enough to survive, perhaps you could come and find us there, if not, then I suppose I would say beware the woods, you may find us still, but not as we are now.

If it is any consolation, my work could be continued as long as the lab remains intact and can be found. Go to the government lab for viral and disease control in the capital and, within the contagious diseases department, look for the work based on an antidote for the undead condition titled 'Zeta 16'. Although this might not be an outright cure, as it remains untested, it may be the nearest thing we have to resisting this plague. Preliminary tests were positive, so there's always a chance.

I have the only sample in existence with me right now and, should I survive tonight, then maybe I'll be able to get it into the right hands. If not, I may be testing it in the field sooner than expected. It may be the only way of saving my family.

I don't know how the outbreak started but I sure hope someone finds a way to end it or this could be the end of human civilisation as we know it. It seems the human race is destined to perish unless someone is willing to make a stand and do something about it.

I am a man of science, but if there is a god, may he have mercy on my soul and the souls of my family and shed some good luck down upon us.

May he bless you too.

Good Luck,

Dr Quentin Colne.

It all came flooding back.

The handwriting was mine! I knew it. It was from me. This was my house.

My name was Quentin Colne.

Hang on. Quentin? What sort of name was that? Hah, Better than Willie Wheels, I suppose.

So, I'd taken the Zeta 16. I'd tried it, I'd tested it and it hadn't worked. I wasn't cured. But it must have done something. All my memories were retained, I wasn't the order following, mindless zombie that everyone else had become, I had become something more. I had become a zombie with individuality, morals, compassion and ideas above my station. And I had passed these on.

Zeta 16 could be our hope for a better unlife; maybe we could reawaken all the memories of all my kin and develop an even better society based on experience and memory and lessons from the past.

Potentially, it held the promise of a longer life for humans as well because if they took it and became infected, yes, they would become zombies, but with all their own memories. Combine this with the regenerative power of the radiation; their bodies would remain reactive and compliant. It could be a form of everlasting life. That was a big concept and I was not sure how the humans would react to that, I would have to put it to them at a future meeting. I know my zombie collective would appreciate the news though. They could all find out who they really were, if it worked. The possibility was intoxicating.

I just hoped there was someone alive that could use this information, know how to work the medical equipment and that the facility was still standing and still contained my work. I could help them make this cure a reality. But I would need help. With my good news in hand, Cyril took me back to the truck. We positioned the reclaimed heads so they could get a good view of the countryside and set off back to our home. This work had to start now. The implications were huge. We could create a whole new race of human-zombie hybrids.

But as we drove away from what was my former life, I felt something for the first time since becoming a zombie.

I felt like myself.
I was me again.
I was Quentin Colne.

Thank-you for buying and reading

We hope you enjoyed it.

If so,
We would be honoured if you leave a review on the Facebook page

www.facebook.com/humanrightsundead

Fishcake Publications
The Independent Publisher with the Author in Mind

Other Books are available from Fishcake Publications
See our website and our webstore at

www.fishcakepublications.com

for information on where to find them.

The following pages are some of latest releases available as paperback and eBook…

Souls of Darkness by Louise Hunt, Damon Rathe and Kenneth Frank

This illustrated book shows exactly what can happen when you take three very different horror, fantasy and sci-fi writers, dismember their work, and then fiendishly stitch it back together in the form of an anthology of their compiled short stories.
A contorted mixture of sinister sci-fi horror, ghostly goings on and true-life terror, carefully combined within the cover of this book.

An anthology of 15 stories / 50,704 words all built around a theme of the darkness within, usually resulting in murder or death. Each story is introduced with an illustration to entice you into what may follow...

Story titles include: River of Dreams, Community Spirits, To Play the Game, Geoff, Shadow of January Gloom, Sensation Seekers, Miss Hate, Redundancy, Eyes in the Dark, Bramble Cottage, Lady Luck, Writer's Block, Disturbance, Just the Three of Us & The Beast.